# The Medallion of Altumeria

Timothy Howard

ISBN:1717478115
ISBN-13: 978-1717478115

# Orran Adventures presents:
## Treasure Hunter Kalia:
## The Medallion of Altumeria

### Welcome to the World of Orran

Welcome to the world of Orran
Four continents on the sea and five in the sky
A world kept in balance not by those who live above ground
But by what lies buried within it.

A world of magic and machinery
Of bronze, brass, copper and tin
Of steam power, Natalie Tesla's coil and sorcery
But most of all... adventure and wonder.

# Orran Skylands

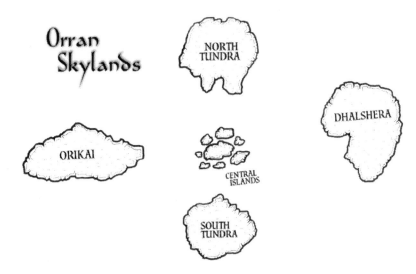

NORTH TUNDRA

DHALSHERA

ORIKAI

CENTRAL ISLANDS

SOUTH TUNDRA

# Orran Sealands

CHIVRALOR

SUVEER-KOTOL

THE UNCHARTABLE ISLES

MASEVRACA

TRICALLIS

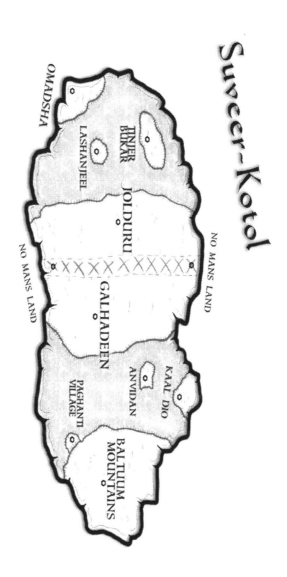
Suveer-Kotol

# Year 112, Era of Invention

For almost one hundred years, the country of Suveer-Kotol had torn itself apart. Following the assassination of Queen Fatillarasa, the already fractious population further descended into civil unrest. A mixture of beliefs and practices caused the kingdom to be divided into two parts.

On the west side sat the Jolduru region, which believed in one god, discipline of the soul and that women should only bear a child, not a title. To the east lay the Galhadeen region, which worshipped many gods and legally practised raising the dead. Whilst Galhadeen boasted superior numbers, Jolduru had better military tactics. In each city is a mile long stretch of abandoned buildings called the evacuated zone. Since stray bullets and units of soldiers can go beyond No Man's Land, where most of the fighting takes place, a large section of the city had to be abandoned for the sake of the civilians. Unfortunately, especially for Galhadeen, many schools were a part of the evacuated zone. The schools that remained in safe territory were not only full but also had to charge tuition fees. If a child's parents didn't earn enough, the child was sent to work in the fields.

*

Six-year-old Kalia Skepali sat on a worn linen blanket, her knees pulled up to her chest. It was night time, and she was camping with her grandfather, Gustaveer. A freshly lit fire cast a warm glow upon their surroundings. Gustaveer had just finished telling Kalia the story of his adventures to the Land of Madness.

"Grandfather, what's over there?" asked Kalia, pointing to a massive rock rise in the far distance.

Gustaveer replied, "The Baltuum Mountains. A treacherous range to climb but rumoured to be filled with vaults of treasure hidden deep within its many caves."

Kalia's eyes widened, her voice excited. "Really! Can you take me one day?"

"I can't. I'm far too old and weak. But there's no reason why you can't go. You were born with two legs. Why not use them to travel the world?"

*

A thirteen-year-old Kalia had just got home from working the fields when her mother, Thaamira, broke the news. Her grandfather was dead.

A mournful silence enveloped the room. Her father, Gashahn, leaned on the table with his head in his hands. Thaamira got up to catch Kalia as she collapsed, weeping. A maelstrom of wretched emotions swarmed her. Kalia felt no energy to stand but her mother's embrace held her upright.

"Do not shoulder any more agony. He died peacefully in his sleep," whispered Thaamira in the Suveerian tongue, a weave of strong Ks and soft Shs.

It provided little comfort.

That night they all sat down for dinner as usual. Thaamira cooked up the best meal she could with what little food they had; boiled kale and beans with a pinch of spice and goat butter. Not a word was spoken during mealtime. Kalia could barely manage her food, pushing it around the bowl and staring at nothing. After dinner they set a circle of candles upon the table. Gashahn lit each one, muttering a prayer under his breath. In the middle of the table he placed a small, pencilled portrait of Gustaveer. It was all anyone had left of Gustaveer's likeness; a face of confidence, neatly combed dark hair and the family birth emblem tattooed across his forehead. Kalia fought back tears as they all prayed in silence with arms crossed and heads bowed.

*"To our many gods who watch over us*
*Please welcome with open arms a dearly departed spirit.*
*Praise be your mercy and compassion*
*And lead him to the final place of rest in your embrace.*
*Gods are many, gods are one*
*Gods are gracious, gods are strong."*

Once finished, Kalia took a single candle upstairs into her cramped quarters without saying a word. Placing the candle by her bedside she crawled into bed, blew out the flame and cried herself to sleep.

\*

The plantation fields; east of Galhadeen city and every child's worst nightmare. But by law, if they weren't in school, they had to work the fields.

Kalia's day started early with a fifteen mile walk to her employer's farmhouse. This was followed by nine hours of laborious harvesting in the baking sun, with a minimal lunch break. Those that didn't work hard enough or disobeyed orders were lashed; twenty across the back with a wicker cane and an additional ten for every further transgression. Repeat offenders were rare.

She was paid a pittance. At least lunch was supplied by her employer, but he wasn't required to. Bread, water and a small piece of fruit for the best workers was the limit of his generosity. During her lunch breaks, Kalia would gaze at the mountains far eastward of the fields with wonder. They were larger than life itself and their copper hue with a blue-sky aura could be seen from miles around. Gustaveer's stories of the treasure and monsters that inhabited their craggy peaks filled her mind.

As she bit into a piece of stale Pitacha bread, a sense of determination filled her body; more so than the scraps of food she had to eat.

*"I was born with two legs, why not use them to explore the world?"* she thought to herself.

"Get back to work!" Mr Bedrio, the field master, yelled.

Kalia closed her eyes, exhaled through her nose and gobbled down the last of her lunch. She turned back to the rows upon rows of coffee shrubs with little enthusiasm.

*

Kalia couldn't leave work fast enough once the bell sounded to signal the end of the day. By the time she reached the city limits her legs felt ready to collapse. Traversing the streets alone was dangerous and stories of kidnappings weren't uncommon. Kalia paced down a set route her father had mapped out, taking her through the most populated streets and roads. The route wasn't the quickest way home, but it was the safest and the sights were better.

Unfortunately, not all the sights were pleasant. Led by a man in expensive silk robes was a group of people in rags and chains. Their pale skin and vacant eyes gave away their predicament. They were reanimations; people brought back from the dead via necromantic rituals. A twisted knot of revulsion tangled in Kalia's stomach. The sight of the reanimated paraded around on the streets reminded her that things could be much, much worse. Putting her discomfort aside, she quickened her pace.

Kalia was halfway home when, to her surprise, she encountered her father in the street, haggling with a merchant for food. Gashahn smiled when he saw her.

"Ah Kalia, pardon me- I will not be a minute," he said.

Kalia watched and listened as her father brought down the price of a bag of rice and spices. In the past she had insisted on putting the money she earned in the fields towards groceries, but Gashahn always smiled and shook his head. *The day you earn more than me is the day you can buy us food,* he would reply.

After the purchase, they strolled down the dusty, dirty streets towards home. Suveerian architecture was considered barbaric by better societies in other well-to-do countries. The buildings were crafted from duststone, which looked like packed mud. Some homes were lucky to have wooden shutters for windows. As a result, civilian living conditions were anything but clean and cosy. The warm climate at least made indoor heating irrelevant even at night, but burglary was commonplace, thanks to poor, insecure design.

"How was work?" asked Gashahn.

"Awful and hard. The days never change," Kalia replied.

"I know that your work is very tiring. I would give anything to see you back at school, or with a better life."

Kalia said nothing and daydreamed about the mountains, scaling their peaks in triumph, plunder in hand.

Evening settled on Galhadeen, casting a dark purple hue on the surroundings. With no gas or teslatronic lighting available, candles were the only source of light in the households. The streets had no illuminative features to speak of. Kalia and Gashahn got home just before the streets became pitch black. No moon glowed in the night sky. Thaamira greeted them at the door.

"Hello my love and beloved," she said.

"Hello my love," said Gashahn, giving her a kiss.

"Did you pick up some cumin and mint?"

"I did indeed. We shall eat tonight."

All three went straight into the kitchen. Along with the two bedrooms, this made up the third room of the house. An outdoor privy stood behind the property. Although there were no doors to the rooms, privacy was always respected.

"Go upstairs and rest if you need to. I will call when dinner is ready," Thaamira said to Kalia.

Kalia ascended the stairs with a candle and was about to throw herself onto her bed when she noticed something sitting on it.

Crafted from dark brown leather with brass clasps and fittings was a backpack. A note sat beside it. Kalia placed the candle by the bedside and brought the note into the light. She was about to call for her mother when she saw what was written on it.

*To Kalia*
*Read the journal*
*Love from Grandfather*

Kalia closed her eyes, crushed the note and held it close to her chest as a mixture of feelings confused her. On one hand she was elated to receive such a gift from her grandfather, but on the other, she was curious as to how the backpack had got here.

The bag was weighty but not too heavy for her. She spread its contents over the bed. Her eyes widened as she created a mental inventory.

First and most notable was a pair of climbing picks tipped with mythril, a light blue metal and the second strongest in the world. Kalia held one in her hand and found its weight perfect in her grip, as if crafted with her in mind.

Second, three thin but very long coils of rope, woven from sisal fibre. The texture wasn't too coarse on her skin and the fibre had some stretch to it.

Next to them lay a flint and tin set for lighting fires. Kalia was starting to see what her grandfather had in mind.

Finally, a leather bound book; her grandfather's journal. Kalia opened it up to the first page and a slip of paper fell out. She picked it up and read it in the warm but dim candlelight.

*'Kalia, if you are reading this then I have passed from this world to join the gods.*
*Though I hold no control over your life, I wish only one thing,*
*I want you to leave this country while you still can.*
*I have left a will but it won't be enough to help you escape*
*And so I pray that what I have left you will give you means to do so.*
*Curse my soul that I could not have made this easier for you.*
*Love from Grandfather.'*

Kalia managed a smile. She'd always felt that she and her grandfather were on the same wavelength. She relaxed onto her bed, leaned against the wall and read the first page of the journal.

*In my lifetime I fought in a pointless war and travelled across the world.*
*I collected many treasures. I have written their final locations in this book and the journey that came with them. These artefacts are worth a fortune in other countries but next to nothing here.*
*I have also written recipes and tips on how to survive in the wilds.*
*Many people never leave Suveer-Kotol, either due to poverty or pride in their country's laws and practices (whatever they may be).*
*I am ashamed to say I remained in Suveer-Kotol for the latter reason.*
*I was full of such foolish pride, fighting for a country that never cared for its people.*
*By the time I had to retire due to the feeble conditions of old age and a broken leg, it was already too late.*
*I had wasted the last third of my life.*
*Now here I sit, writing memoirs of my youth; the only time I didn't waste.*

Thaamira called up to Kalia for dinner. Kalia folded up the note and used it as a bookmark, even though she had only finished the first page.

At the dinner table the Skepalis ate a meal of spiced rice. No vegetables or meat accompanied the food, as these had been finished the night before and neither could be afforded at the best of times. Gashahn and Thaamira spoke of work until Kalia found a pause in the conversation.

"What did Grandfather do before he joined the army?"

Both parents looked at her in surprise.

"I have no idea. He never spoke of his life before he joined the fighting. Why do you ask?" answered Gashahn.

Kalia hesitated to make up an answer. "He used to tell me about the adventures he had. Do you think he was an explorer or a freelance adventurer?"

Thaamira gave a nervous smile. "Kalia, your grandfather made up those stories to keep you amused as a child."

The answer silenced Kalia. *"They don't know about the backpack."*

After dinner, Kalia kissed her parents goodnight and bounded upstairs to her room. The candle there was melted halfway down but still had plenty of wick and wax left for a day or two. Kalia changed into a nightgown, stuffed everything back into the bag and then shoved it under her pillow. She didn't want her parents to know about Grandfather's gift…yet.

\*

Gashahn and Thaamira sat at the dinner table, sipping water as they looked over a will written on dusty, browned parchment.

"One thousand iritons… is that enough to get Kalia out of the country?" Thaamira asked Gashahn, keeping her voice low.

"No, but give it a few months and we can save up enough for travel." Gashahn shrugged and looked away, also holding back the volume of his voice. "That's if we can find a ship that'll take her."

Thaamira ran a hand through her hair then leaned on the table, chin resting in the palm of her hand. "I'm sick of her living like this. Little girls shouldn't be forced to work in a field."

Gashahn looked at her. "Hundreds of others do."

"I know, I know... Do you remember the first time I found those cane scars on her back? I wanted to scream."

"You said you wanted to kill Mr Bedrio. I wanted to lend a hand," Gashahn said with a half-cocked smile.

Thaamira shook her head. "Where should we send her? I hear Masevraca has a warm climate."

"We might not have a choice, she could end up in Tricallis. It'll still be better than here."

"Do you think she'll want to go? Leaving us behind?"

Gashahn downed the water in his cup. "Letting her go will be the hardest part." He stood up. "Tomorrow I'm going to ask for an advance on my payment. I should get it if I tell them the circumstances." He held out his hand to Thaamira. "Shall we sleep on it for tonight?"

Thaamira finished her drink and took the hand.

*

Kalia sat cross-legged and leaned up against the wall as she opened up the journal's first chapter.

## The Suveerian Treasures

*I was nineteen years old. Myself, Anwar and Uwais had just returned from north Tricallis. It was an excursion rife with humid temperatures and tiny blood-sucking insects. We had collected a few trinkets made from gold, silver and obsidian and upon returning, we devised a plan to keep them safe. We could have sold them, but felt the items were worth more to the right buyer, preferably one in a different country to our own. At least that's what I told my friends. A day after we made shore a boy approached me. How he knew of my treasure- hunting exploits I do not know, but he was well dressed and terrified. He gave me a small wooden box and begged me to keep it safe. I gave him my word just to get him to go away, but when I looked inside the box I saw a medallion. It was not just any medallion, it was made of the purest gold I had ever seen and I swear in the shaded space of the box, it irradiated an aura of light. A strange sensation made me feel more obliged to keep my promise.*

*So myself, Anwar and Uwais packed our bags with our spoils and ancient family heirlooms. We set out for Paghanti village upon rented filjinahs, the Baltuum Mountains our destination. In times spanning back to the Savage Era the Baltuum Mountains served as a perilous yet secure vault. People would traverse the mountains and then dig their own caves to safe-keep their valuables. How high and deep into the mountain range they travelled determined the security of their belongings. Foolishly, myself and my friends travelled perhaps too far in search of the perfect hiding place.*

Before she could read any more, the sound of footsteps came from the stairs. Kalia shoved the book under the pillow, blew out the candle and tucked herself under the covers before her parents reached the top of the stairs.

*

Four hooded figures walked into a tavern. They didn't order drinks but strode up to a table tucked away in a corner. The bar was empty, save for a portly bartender wiping down the counter, unnerved by the four mysterious individuals. Despite the rough neighbourhood, the place was kept clean and tidy. The seats against the walls were separated by wooden barriers carved with shapes of plumes and flourishes. A single hanging oil lantern was the only light source, meaning everything in the corners was enveloped in shadow.

Minutes passed before a man in his late thirties with thick stubble walked in. He gave a nervous wave to the bartender, who timidly nodded back. The man spotted the four figures and approached their table.

One of the four turned towards the man. He wore a long, hooded robe and a gilded mask shaped like an expressionless human face, a ruby encrusted on the forehead. Presumably the leader of the group, he spoke with a cold, detached voice that echoed behind his face of gold.

"Shatysh, I trust you have agreed to our terms?"

Shatysh ran a hand through his hair and tried to steady his voice as he spoke. "Yes, in exchange for safe passage out of the country."

The Leader said nothing, his eyes not visible behind the mask. He drew a small card out of thin air and handed it to Shatysh, the stencil of a birth emblem drawn upon it.

"Find the family who bears this birth emblem. They possess a pure gold medallion that does not belong to them. Learn of its location, then kill them."

Shatysh struggled to stop his hand from shaking as he held the card.

He recognised the tattoo.

*

Dull sunlight peeked through the shutters of Kalia's bedroom window. The blankets she slept on provided little comfort. Kalia slowly pushed herself out of bed against the strain of her aching muscles and went downstairs for breakfast, leaving her backpack and book hidden underneath the pillow.

A meal of Pitacha bread and goat butter welcomed her to the table. Gashahn had already left for work.

Her mother leaned on the counter drinking from an aged clay cup. Her job at the silk factory didn't start for another hour.

"Morning," Thaamira said with a smile.

"Morning, Mother," Kalia smiled back.

Kalia took a seat at the table and wolfed down her breakfast. The Pitacha bread was bland but the goat butter added a nice creamy flavour; an affordable Suveerian breakfast.

With a mouthful of food, Kalia plotted out her day. She wanted to tackle the mountain, find the treasure and use the funds to help secure her family a better life. She didn't care how childish and hopeful this sounded. Thinking of the journal inspired a confident sense of adventure within her.

"Mother, may I take some food with me to work today?" Kalia never usually asked this, but she needed the extra supplies for the journey.

"I can cook you some rice to take just before you leave."

Kalia smiled through the feeling of guilt. "Thank you, Mother."

"Take some water up to wash with. I'll have your rice ready shortly."

Kalia kissed her mother on the cheek, fetched a bowl of water and raced upstairs, taking care not to spill a drop. She splashed her face then scrubbed up for the day. She dressed in one of the few outfits she owned; a pale green, loose-fitting garment, a light blue head scarf and a pair of sandals.

Kalia looked towards her pillow, plotting a way to get the backpack downstairs and out of the house without her mother noticing.

*"Or, I could just let her see what Grandfather left for me and explain that I'm going on a journey to the mountains in search of treasure...? Perhaps not..."*

Kalia stuffed the journal in the backpack, picked it up and slowly paced downstairs. Once there, she placed the backpack in the hallway, out of her mother's sight. She snuck a peek into the kitchen where her mother was focused on stirring the contents of a boiling copper pot. A small kindling fire surrounded by stone guards and holds provided the heat. Instinctively Kalia grabbed the bag and moved it closer to the front door. Her mother didn't notice. Walking into the kitchen, Kalia put on her best look of innocence and stood beside her mother.

Thaamira glanced quickly at Kalia and smiled. "Almost ready."

After a minute more of cooking, Thaamira drained the pot into a tin colander then fetched a skin, made from a goat's stomach. She stuffed the skin with fluffy white rice and tightened the drawstring.

Thaamira handed over the lunch bag. "Try not to lose it," she said with a smile.

Kalia took it and hugged her mother tightly. "Thank you."

With a wave, Kalia left the kitchen, picking up the backpack on her way out of the house.

When she was far enough away from home, Kalia shoved the rice skin into the bag.

*

Kalia walked with intent, eastwards to the fields. At this time in the morning, most people were in bed. Shops and stalls wouldn't open for another hour. Kalia spotted around two or three other kids stepping out of their homes, some half asleep, others miserable as they walked with hunched shoulders whilst staring at the ground. By the time she reached the city limits, some store owners had started rigging up their wooden stalls and worn banners.

Every morning, around thirty minutes after she started work, a large delivery steam truck would pass the fields. Kalia's plan was to hitch a ride on the truck. She just needed it to stop long enough for her to get aboard.

The children, her fellow field workers, were already gathered outside when she reached the farmhouse. The smell of crisp stone and sweat from the city was replaced by an overwhelming punch of bitter coffee plants and soil.

Kalia found her friend Hasana leaning against the farmhouse wall, playing with the strands from the overhanging hay-thatched roof. Hasana stood a little taller than Kalia but had shorter hair and her birth emblem across her collarbone. It looked like a bird with outstretched wings, but with a more abstract design.

"Hey Hasana," Kalia said with a wave.

"Hey Kalia," Hasana smiled when she saw her.

Kalia approached her friend and whispered, "I need a favour."

Hasana groaned. "What is it this time?"

"Well, you know the steam truck that passes our field? I need to hitch a ride on it."

Hasana's eyes widened. "Are you crazy? How many lashes is Mr Bedrio going to give you if you're caught?"

"Thirty, but it'll be worth it."

"What could possibly be worth thirty lashes?"

Kalia looked over towards the mountain range and pointed. "Let's just say I have other places to be."

Hasana blinked and rubbed her temple. "Look, I can help, but try not to cry too hard into my shoulder if this goes wrong."

"If this goes right, I won't ever need to cry again."

Hasana shuffled her feet and looked at the ground, deep in contemplation. "So how are we going to get you on the truck?"

"Let me worry about getting on the truck. I need you to stop it."

"The old 'pass out from illness' trick?"

"Perfect. Thanks again."

"Hey, where did you get that backpack?"

Kalia paused and looked at the shoulder strap, wondering if she could keep the bag on whilst working. "My grandfather gave it to me," she explained.

The rusty hinged door to the farmhouse opened and Mr Bedrio ambled out. He was a ragged, lanky man with a beard that expanded out from his face but not underneath his nose. He wore a creased, stained, linen shirt and a waistcoat with a light dusting of dirt. He bellowed orders and handed out water skins to each child.

Once he had finished barking, everyone walked to their assigned field without question. He didn't pass comment on Kalia's new accessory.

Allocated to her usual field and with a hoe in hand, Kalia got to work on an empty patch. A boy planted seeds as she shaped the soil into shallow trenches. The heat of the sun made the work sweltering. Hasana worked a few metres away.

Eventually, the growl of an old steam engine reached Kalia's ears.

"Hasana, it's coming. Are you ready?"

"I… don't feel so good…" Hasana held her stomach and stumbled towards the road, giving Kalia a wink on the way.

Hasana reached the road where the steam truck was about to pass. In the middle, she dropped to her knees, then collapsed onto her front. The steam truck trundled down the lane, thick black smoke billowing from its chimney. It slowed down to a stop in front of Hasana's body. Two men jumped out of the truck to attend the supposedly sick girl.

Kalia glanced around to make sure she wasn't being watched, then crept to the back of the truck's cargo hold. The truck's bronze body was smeared with corrosion and the cargo hold's tarpaulin cover was a filthy brown-beige colour. Pulling aside the rear curtain cover, she saw that the back container was packed full of crates. Kalia would have to climb up in order to hide away.

She looked for an edge to grab onto. The top of the crate was high up, but it was the only ledge she could see.

Kalia jumped up, found a grip and pulled herself up. Her foot slipped but she found her balance, ignored the flush of embarrassment and hauled herself up and on top of the crates. She rolled along further into the truck's hold; there was little space as the crates were stacked almost to the ceiling.

As she lay silent in the gap between the top of the crate and the roof, she could hear the voice of Mr Bedrio.

"What is going on here?" Mr Bedrio's voice drew closer, loud and irritated.

"This child appeared in front of us and collapsed in the middle of the road," said one of the drivers.

"She's being lazy again. You! Get up and get back to work unless you want the cane," yelled Mr Bedrio.

"Yes sir, sorry sir."

After a moment of silence, Kalia heard the *ker-clump* of doors closing. The vehicle trembled as the engine started. Kalia felt the steam truck pull away and let out a sigh of relief. A warm but soft draught flowed across her.

*"No turning back,"* she thought as she peeked through the curtains and watched the scenery pass by.

*

The steam truck drove on for hours. Kalia kept an eye out to try and keep track of where she was. The vehicle travelled far beyond the fields and Kalia felt every bump from the potholes in the road. She wanted to sleep, but knew she would have to make a quick exit when the vehicle stopped.

To pass the time, she read her grandfather's journal.

*From Paghanti village we traversed a steep hill that led to the base of the mountain. At the top of the hill was a vertical wall we had to climb. I remember climbing for half an hour before I reached a ledge. Myself and my friends agreed to move eastwards alongside the mountain. We eventually reached a crevasse, separating our mountain from another. Full of vigour and courage we agreed to cross it. We were smart enough to pack some supplies just for this task. Anwar got to work, hammering in a pair of rock spikes whilst I prepared to make the jump to the other side. Tying a rope around my waist, I gave the other end to Uwais, who secured it to Anwar's rock spike, leaving at least ten coils loose. I made it across, only barely making the ledge, though Uwais and Anwar applauded my efforts. We made a rope crossing and continued upwards along the mountain path.*

*The path narrowed until we had to sidestep yet again but widened when we reached another chasm. This jump was shorter but the ridge was further down. We made it without any trouble or the need for a bridge but left a rock spike and a single hanging coil of rope. As we walked along the path of the third mountain we questioned how far we were willing to travel just to find our strongroom.*

Kalia stopped reading; she needed to keep an eye on her surroundings. The motion sickness didn't help. Her view through a gap in the tarpaulin showed only the countryside. She had no idea what the vehicle's final destination would be, only that it was going west.

Eventually the truck slowed down. Kalia spotted a sign but couldn't make it out through the tiny view hole. When the truck stopped for a second, Kalia peeked past the curtain. With the coast clear, she climbed down and grunted as she extended her arms to stretch. Kalia recognised the surroundings of single floor shacks, some made from duststone whilst others were hastily put together with scrap tin sheets. Every building had hay-thatched roofs. Kalia was in Paghanti village.

Despite its secure location, the village made a living by developing munitions for the army; originally a task for the seaside town of Kaal Dio until a horrific accident left the town in ruin.

Kalia didn't need long to gather her bearings. The Baltuum Mountains were almost immeasurable in size, they were so close to the village. It took all her focus not to stand on the spot and gawp.

Kalia ducked into a nearby alleyway to get off the street. There was a wobble in her step from the restless journey. Mud spread up the walls of the lane and the stench of acrid chemicals hung in the air. The entire village was plagued with the smell. Kalia covered her nose with her head wrap but her stomach still felt discomforted.

Kalia passed across the next street, avoiding the human traffic. Her stomach felt even worse when she realised some of the inhabitants were reanimated slaves.

After passing north from a triangular junction, with a pile of junk in the centre, she finally reached the path to the mountain base. It ran up a steep hill and Kalia could see where it ended and became a wall of flaked mineral. Her stomach grumbled. It was just past noon, so she found a secluded spot and fished out the skin of rice her mother had made for her. Having scooped a single handful into her mouth, she tightened the bag's drawstring and placed it in her backpack. She needed to be sparing with her food.

After washing down the rice with a drink of water from the skin Mr Bedrio had so generously given her, Kalia ascended the hill.

As Paghanti village trailed further behind her, the nasty smell faded and she found breathing to be a much more pleasant experience. She needed that breath for the climb.

The slope was paved with loose gravel and Kalia slipped three times trying to scale the hill. At the top stood the wall to the mountain.

The cliff-side was pocked with holes, crevices and ledges. Kalia gripped the ledge above her; the stone smooth and warm under her fingers. Her sandals, however, were not up to the task of climbing and although she found purchase on every ledge, it felt awkward and unsecure.

As Kalia climbed, she breathed in the cleanest air she had ever tasted. The very scent of the mountain exhilarated her. She ascended with a new-found energy and a smile on her face.

She hadn't felt happiness like this in a long time.

The climb was long and doubt crept into her mind, making Kalia question if this treasure hunt was a good idea. She was forty feet up but dared not look down.

Eventually Kalia found a long narrow ledge and quickened her pace.

Once into position, she sidestepped eastwards, grabbing anything she could to keep herself fixed to the mountainside. Yet again, the journey around the peak was long.

The second mountain came into view, but by the time Kalia had reached the chasm crossing, her joints and back felt stiff.

Kalia rested against the rocks. The path had widened, giving her room to stretch. She gauged the distance across but made a mistake; she looked down. The depth of the chasm made Kalia pull back and stumble. She clutched the stone behind her, hyperventilating.

Kalia closed her eyes and breathed deeply. She exhaled in timed, shorts bursts. *'One... Two... Three.'* She repeated this three times and it helped to bring her breathing under control.

Kalia opened her backpack to fetch one coil of rope and her mythril picks. Scanning around she found two bronze rock spikes. They had been corroded by time, but a nudge from her foot found both spikes secured in the stone.

It occurred to Kalia that she wasn't an expert in knot tying. She sat cross legged and pulled the journal out of her backpack. Consulting a contents page at the front of the book, she found a section on knots, complete with hand drawn diagrams. Her grandfather's artwork was detailed, but Kalia still struggled to tie her cable around the spike.

Giving the rope a few tugs to check it was secure, Kalia wrapped the cord around her waist, ensuring she left ten coils spare. Binding the loop wasn't as difficult this time around.

Kalia faced the other mountain and made one final check: Her ropes were secure, her backpack was strapped to her body and she had a mythril pick in each hand.

She darted forwards and leapt.

She made it halfway across.

Something went wrong. Perhaps, as she jumped, doubt made her falter or she slipped on a smooth rocky surface.

She plummeted, screaming.

Kalia's body tumbled through the air at a frightening speed. She clutched her picks and swung wildly, trying to find something solid to latch onto. There was nothing.

Kalia came to an abrupt stop in mid-air, the rope around her waist crushing her stomach and straining her spine. The momentum swung her into the mountain wall behind her. She bounced off, cracking her elbow in the process. In a panic, she dropped both her picks. Pain shot through Kalia's body as she hung helplessly from the cable. She missed the opportunity to latch onto the mountainside; it was too steep and smooth to climb with her bare hands. Tears welled in her eyes. She couldn't climb back up the rope- her right arm was in too much pain.

Wiping her tears, she grabbed on with her left hand and tried to pull herself up.

A *thwip* sound came from above and the cable shot out with it.

Kalia disappeared into the abyss.

*

Gashahn rushed through the front door and into the kitchen. Thaamira turned to face him, her eyes wide with surprise.

"My beloved! What's happening?" she asked.

"I-I received a message from a work colleague. He told me there was an emergency at home. Is everything ok?"

"Everything is fine. I received the same message. I thought that Kalia…"

There was a knock at the door. Gashahn and Thaamira looked towards the hallway. Gashahn slowly paced over to the kitchen window. He opened the shutters quietly and poked his head outside.

"Shatysh! Hello friend," Gashahn called with a smile.

Gashahn closed the shutters behind him and invited Shatysh inside. They exchanged pleasantries before making themselves comfortable at the kitchen table. Thaamira remained standing.

"Hello Shatysh, what brings you to our door?" she asked.

Shatysh ran a hand through his hair. "Umm… I have a friend who specialises in curios and relics. He mentioned that the… ancestors who bear your birth emblem were in possession… of an angelic medallion."

"That's… interesting," said Gashahn. "So why are you here?"

"This friend said… that the angelic medallion is worth two million iritons. Enough to get both of our families out of this country, away from the war."

Thaamira spoke up. "So you think we have it?"

Shatysh stopped smiling. "Yes, or at least know of its location."

Gashahn got up from his seat and poured himself a drink of water. "I am sorry Shatysh," he sipped from the cup; the water had a strong metallic taste, "but we don't have anything of that value and we don't know of its location, not unless my father ever found one, but he... recently passed away." Gashahn glanced at Thaamira. "We're still grieving. I'm sorry we couldn't be of more assistance but we should be getting back to work. Which reminds me, I didn't get that advance on my wages. My boss is... quite angry with me."

Thaamira gave a limp smile whilst returning Gashahn's gaze.

Shatysh gazed vacantly down at the table. He slowly got to his feet. "I am sorry to hear that, but never mind. It's good to see you both again."

Gashahn extended his hand. "You too, neighbour."

Shatysh placed a hand on Gashahn's shoulder. With the other hand, he stabbed Gashahn in the stomach. It happened quickly, with a small, concealed blade.

Thaamira stood still in shock for a few seconds before the weight of the situation hit her and she reacted instinctively. Her face twisting with rage, she picked up the chair her husband had been sitting on. Swinging it as hard as she could, Thaamira smashed the chair into Shatysh's head. The chair splintered and snapped into pieces and the blow sent Shatysh to the floor.

Thaamira rushed to attend her husband. Blood leaked from his wound and he was struggling to breathe. She removed her veil and pressed it up against the gash, then turned to Shatysh.

"What is wrong with you?" Thaamira screamed.

She saw him reach for the blade.

Thaamira grabbed a broken chair leg, stepped on Shatysh's hand and held the sharp end of her weapon to his throat.

"Who sent you?"

Shatysh grunted. The sound of footsteps came from the hallway.

Out of the corner of Thaamira's eye, she saw someone stalk into the kitchen. The figure's appearance made her breathing stop for a second. He wore a grey hooded robe with silver trim and a mask of gold. He held a gleaming, flexentite backsword with a golden basket hilt. Thaamira turned her weapon towards him.

There was no chance to use it before the masked man lunged forward with a speed Thaamira couldn't keep up with. The sword ran through her chest. She tried to raise her arm but found no strength to lift it. The stake of wood fell from her grasp. The blade was removed from her heart before she collapsed to the floor.

Shatysh crawled up from his position and leaned against the wall.

Holding his wound tightly, Gashahn stumbled towards his wife, but he, too, was met with a sword through the heart. The masked man's skill and precision with the weapon made Shatysh gawp.

Gashahn's body collapsed next to his wife's.

"Be thankful no one else is around. Now what did you learn?" The man in the gilded mask demanded of Shatysh, his voice pitiless and stiff.

"They do not know where it is. Gashahn mentioned his father may have found one but his secret went to the grave with him."

The masked man paused "Fine. You have done well."

Shatysh nodded. "So, what arrangements have you made to help me leave?"

He was answered with a blank stare, followed by bloodied flexentite metal through his chest.

Shatysh couldn't manage a word before he stopped moving.

Seconds later, three other cloaked individuals entered the house. The Leader picked up Thaamira's stained veil and wiped his blade on a dry patch before addressing them.

"Search the house. Thoroughly." He made a quick count of the bodies. "There's one missing."

*

Kalia's eyes opened. Agony pulsed through her limbs. Even the slightest movement triggered a chain reaction of pain. Purple and red bruises covered her dark brass skin. She lay upon a bed of folded blankets, similar to her sleeping arrangement at home. A quick observation revealed the room around her to be made of loosely fitted palm wood planks. Sunlight streamed through the gaps. Someone stirred a copper pot over a duststone fireplace; a man in his late thirties. He wore a square scarfed headdress called a keffiyeh, a pair of long, loose, dirt coloured slacks and a folded cotton upper garment. The man was a Sherpa, an expert explorer of the mountains.

"You're lucky to be alive," said the Sherpa without turning around. "If I hadn't found you, the wolves certainly would have."

"W-Where am I?" Kalia asked weakly.

"You are inside my house at the base of the Baltuum Mountains, north-west of Paghanti village."

"Who are you?"

"I am commonly known as the Baltuum Sherpa. You may call me the Sherpa. By what name shall I call you?"

"I'm… Kalia. How did you find me?"

"You ask many questions. Do I at least get some gratitude?"

Kalia remembered her manners. "Thank you. You saved my life."

The Sherpa glanced over at Kalia. He had a full-face beard but his birth emblem wasn't visible. He nodded and smiled. "I have travelled the mountains for many years. The bottom of the ravine you fell into is easy to get to from the ground. Had you fallen anywhere else, you might have died. Now I must ask a question in kind: what were you doing climbing the Baltuum Mountains?"

Kalia brought herself up to a seated position, though she winced through the aches in her body. "I… wanted to get away from working the fields."

Using a tin ladle, the Sherpa filled a clay bowl with a thick, grey, gruel or soup-like mixture. Kalia wasn't sure what it was until she tasted it. Mushroom soup; probably the best she'd ever tasted. It was creamy and full of flavour.

The Sherpa sat cross-legged next to Kalia and checked her right arm.

"You landed hard on your arm. Your climbing equipment is over there in the corner. It is good quality, but your attire is not."

Kalia looked away and said nothing.

"I can understand why you left the fields, but do you have parents?"

Again Kalia said nothing, but gave a small nod.

"And do they not love you?"

"Yes," whispered Kalia.

"Think of them the next time you run away."

The Sherpa arose and walked over to his cooking pot to pour himself a bowl of soup. Once Kalia had finished her meal, she tried to stand up. Her right knee throbbed and at first she struggled to put weight on it, but she managed to limp over to her backpack in the corner. She found certain movements less painful and grimaced as she slung the rucksack over her back.

"Are you local to Paghanti village?" asked the Sherpa.

"No, I live in southeast Galhadeen."

The Sherpa did a double take. "Then how did you get here?"

"I… stowed away on a delivery truck."

The Sherpa shook his head. "It's getting late. I doubt you can get back to the city before the land turns dark. I cannot help you with transport, but if you leave now you might be able to hide aboard a delivery truck again. One leaves the village at six o' clock."

"Thank you," said Kalia as she hobbled out of the shack.

The sun was still bright in the sky but appeared moments away from disappearing below the horizon. The border of Paghanti village could be seen south of the Sherpa's shack. Kalia limped towards the village, sucking in air to numb the pain.

*

Kalia caught sight of a familiar steam truck; it was the same one she had arrived in. She quickened her step. Someone sat in the passenger seat, surveying the surroundings. Kalia ambled around to the back of the vehicle, her breathing laboured from fatigue and agony.

There were fewer boxes this time around, so Kalia had less of a struggle climbing inside. She found a niche corner tucked away behind a stack of boxes and hid there. A minute later and the clunk of a door shutting followed by the engine growling signalled to Kalia that her second stowaway attempt had been successful. Either security checks were too relaxed or the drivers just didn't care. It didn't matter, As Kalia clutched her knees to her chest, she told herself this would be the last time.

To pass the time, she fetched her grandfather's journal once more.

*

As the Sherpa predicted, the steam truck arrived in Galhadeen as the landscape engulfed itself in darkness. Kalia crawled out from behind her hiding space to get a better view of the passing scenery.

As soon as the truck trundled to a slow pace, Kalia jumped out onto the street; a move she regretted, as a sharp, stinging pain shot up her leg, making her whimper and stumble.

Kalia scanned the street. The moon illuminated the sides and surfaces of buildings, but she didn't recognise any landmarks.

Kalia sighed and shook her head. She was about to ask for directions when a police officer turned and marched towards her. He wore a tin plated fez embedded with a gold badge, and a cloth veil covered his ears and the back of his neck. His uniform consisted of a brown jacket adorned with felt pauldrons, a silver aiguillette and a tulwar sabre. Kalia considered turning and running, but the officer had a hand on her shoulder before she could act. He held up a small, copper, bullseye lantern and examined the birth emblem on Kalia's forehead.

"Miss Skepali?" he asked.

"Y-Yes?"

"I need you to come with me," he demanded with a severe expression.

"I-I'm sorry... I..."

"Now! You are needed at home."

Home... the image of Kalia's parents, full of anger and disappointment, filled her mind. The thought of the scolding she was soon to receive made her cringe.

The policeman grabbed Kalia's arm and dragged her along with a firm grip. She whined and hobbled in protest. Her body still hurt from the accident and she struggled to keep up, but the officer ignored her.

When they reached the street where Kalia lived, there was a rabble of people outside her home. The officer ordered them all to move aside and return to their houses.

The crowd looked at Kalia, faces full of sorrow and shock. They parted as she came closer.

Kalia saw sheets covering two prone forms in the centre of the crowd.

Tears streamed down her face as she approached the sheets. Her legs shook as she knelt down.

*"No."*

Her hands quivered as she reached for the top of one of the covers.

*"P-Please... no."*

Her breath stammered as she peeled back the cover...

... and saw the pale face of her mother.

Kalia screamed so loudly that everyone flinched and so hard that her throat felt like it was tearing itself apart. Her eyes sealed shut as tears flowed from them.

Kalia pressed her face against her dead mother's shoulder and tightly wrapped her arms around the body. No warmth or comfort came from the embrace.

A pair of hands gripped Kalia's shoulders, aggressively pulling her away. She could hear the policeman barking orders, but she couldn't make them out. The commands sounded so distant.

*"Anything. Anything but this,"* her thoughts repeated over and over.

The world slowed down. Distorted noises rang out and surrounded her as she cocooned herself from the world.

*

Kalia curled up on her bed space, her face damp from tears. All the cuts, bruises and torn muscles she'd suffered didn't hurt so much anymore. Her head felt cloudy and pulsated like a heartbeat. She had cried so much she was dehydrated. The military police were of no help; the officer that dragged her home had ordered her to go inside without sympathy, then left.

A knock at the front door barely made her budge.

"Kalia, are you in?" came Hasana's voice from downstairs, calling through the letter box.

Kalia turned her head towards her bedroom doorway.

"Kalia it's me. Please let me in."

Kalia crawled out of bed, lit the candle by her bedside and brought it along as she slowly shuffled downstairs. She placed the candle on the hallway shelf as she opened the front door.

Hasana stood there, unsmiling. She nearly broke down as she held Kalia in a hug. Only after kicking the door shut did they both burst into tears, crying into each other's shoulders.

A minute later, Hasana led Kalia to the kitchen table. No trace of the carnage that had previously stained the room remained. Kalia took a seat and leant on the table with her head in both arms. Hasana fetched two clay cups of water.

"Here, drink this," said Hasana as she placed a hand on Kalia's shoulder. "I'm here for you now."

"Thank you, my friend," said Kalia, her voice still raspy and weak. She sipped from her drink. "The city council told me I have until morning before this house is taken back." She frowned and sniffed as she clenched her cup tightly. "Apparently I'm too young to own this house."

Hasana lips took a downturn. "I'm sorry."

Kalia looked at her friend. "For what?"

"I asked my mother if you could stay with us, but we struggle to make a living as it is and… and we wouldn't be able to feed you or…" Hasana trailed off and the room fell silent again.

Eventually Kalia cleared her throat and spoke up. "Don't worry. I'll be fine."

Hasana wiped away another tear. "But what will you do? How will you live?"

Kalia gulped down the rest of her drink. "I'm leaving this country. My mum and dad were the only people I cared about and the only reason I had to stay here. Now they're gone…" her voice wavered and she swallowed. "I have no reason to be here. I'm going back to the mountains and I'm going to find my grandfather's treasure."

Surprisingly, Hasana didn't appear shocked. Instead she smiled. "Then let's get you started. How can I help?"

Kalia looked down at herself and what she was wearing. "I'm going to need a change of clothes."

They scurried upstairs. Hasana lit another candle and looked around in Kalia's room. Kalia stood in the hallway, gazing at her parent's room. *"Mum, Dad, forgive me…"* She breathed deeply, exhaled and entered the bedroom.

Gashaan and Thaamira's bedroom was only a few square metres larger than Kalia's room, with a double blanket folded on the floor for a bed and a wide chest of drawers.

Kalia emptied both drawers out onto the bed. She rummaged around the pile of clothes and found a pair of her father's white sirwals; baggy trousers. She slipped them on and despite the pants being long in the leg, the drawstring tightened to Kalia's waist. She folded up the bottoms of the legs and picked up another pair, stuffing them into her backpack. As she opened the bag she spotted the skin of rice her mother had given her, surprisingly still intact. Kalia lifted up the bag and gazed at it; the last thing her mother had given her. Kalia refrained from shedding any more tears and put the skin back in the rucksack.

Kalia threw off her veil and robe as Hasana entered with a bundle of clothes.

"Here's all I could find," said Hasana as she dumped Kalia's clothes onto a space on the bed.

"Thank you. I'm going to need clothes that won't get in my way."

"Hmm… what about your father's shirts?"

Kalia shook her head. "They won't fit me."

Hasana paused to think for a second then clicked her fingers as an idea came to her. "What if we took one of your robes, cut it off at the waist, then stitched up the fabric where it frays?"

Kalia nodded her head. "Yes that sounds like it might work. Hold on whilst I fetch a few things."

With a candle in hand, Kalia stepped downstairs into the kitchen. A quick search in the drawers revealed a spool of thread, a needle and some scissors. Once back upstairs, she picked out a deep red garment and threw it on.

Hasana poked around to find Kalia's waist then cut into the dress, carefully snipping around Kalia by pulling the fabric away from her body.

Once the lower part of the dress was cut away, they both began sewing. Kalia pulled off the dress and handed Hasana a spare needle. They folded up the frayed fabric then sealed it with a needle and thread, guided only by the dim candlelight.

Hasana and Kalia worked in silence but displayed content smiles to each other at times. Once the seam was finished, Kalia slid the shirt back on and gave a twirl.

"How do I look?" Kalia asked.

Hasana paused with her hand on her chin before responding. "Different. I'm not sure how the authorities will react to a woman wearing manly clothes."

"I'll pack a spare robe and change into my new clothes when I'm out of sight."

"Are you sure this is what you want to do? I mean... leave on a treasure hunt? Is the treasure even worth anything?"

"Oh, the treasure's worth a lot. In my grandfather's journal, he mentions they stored trinkets made of gold, silver and obsidian."

Hasana's jaw slackened. "Wow, that's more than what most people have around here."

"That's why this journey is worth it." Kalia looked out at the night sky through the window. "I almost quit after the first time. That's how I got these bruises. I felt that as long as I had my parents... I could put up with life here..." Kalia's head drooped. She closed her eyes as tears dewed on her lashes.

Hasana held her close in a hug and whispered in her ear, "I'll be here if you ever want to come back."

Kalia clasped Hasana's hand and managed a weak smile. "Thank you. May I ask another favour?"

"Of course."

"Can you stay here for the night? I've never spent a night alone in the house and-"

"It's fine. I will stay the night here with you. Let's clean up this mess, we've got an early start in the morning."

They stitched up the leg hems on Kalia's sirwals for safety and convenience. Before the two retired to bed, Kalia set up a circle of candles on the kitchen table. She lit each one and placed a pencilled portrait in the middle. The picture was of Kalia, Thaamira and Gashaan during much happier times. Kalia herself had been just a toddler at the time.

Though Kalia would never admit it out loud for fear of punishment, she'd never cared for any religious practice or belief. Devout ideals were but one of the triggers that started the war in the first place, but she performed the ritual of passing regardless. Her parents always held true to the practice and in their honour, so would she.

Kalia and Hasana knelt at the table. With arms crossed and heads bowed they prayed just as Kalia had done for her grandfather.

Kalia blew out the candles, save for one which she kept for light. Hasana followed her upstairs and once settled, she extinguished the flame so that they could rest.

*

Kalia stood atop a mountain, gazing down at her parent's house. Despite what felt like hundreds of miles between herself and them, she could make them out, waving and smiling with pride.

A hollow sensation in her gut made her run at full speed down the mountainside, where it was steep, but traversable.

Kalia ran with tears flowing from her eyes. She couldn't care less about the distance, she was going to reach them.

Halfway down the mountain, her lungs began to burn. Kalia sprinted faster, not wanting to be outdone by her body's limits.

She reached the bottom, her body shaking from the strain and her hands on her knees. She glanced up and saw her parents, miles from her position.

Kalia gritted her teeth and sprinted once more, choking back tears and sobs.

Her parents came closer. Thaamira knelt down and opened up her arms, ready to sweep Kalia up in a hug. One mile left. Kalia screamed for her mother and father.

When she was ten or so yards from them, she slowed down, so as not to bowl them over.

But then she saw them, still as statues.

Kalia's pace slowed further. Her jaw clenched as she shook her head.

Thaamira and Gashahn disintegrated like grains of sand in the wind.

Kalia dropped to her knees, paralysed by the reality as her world went black.

*

Kalia awoke shivering, pale light illuminating her surroundings. She turned over to see Hasana sleeping peacefully beside her.

Kalia blenched as she pulled herself up, crept over to the window and opened its shutters. The morning sun's rays could be seen over the roof tops, but the surrounding streets were still shrouded in dark purple hues.

Kalia turned back and dressed into her climbing clothes and a light blue veil, throwing a pale green robe over the top to cover up her questionable fashion choice; at least in everyone else's opinion.

She realised she still needed a decent pair of shoes for climbing.

In a corner of the bedroom were pairs of her parents' shoes, including her father's loafers. She slipped her foot into one but, unsurprisingly, it didn't fit. She had an idea when she looked over at her parents' clothing stacks, which had been neatly folded by herself and Hasana last night. She picked out a baggy robe from her own stack of clothes and cut off part of the sleeve. She then lined the inside of the loafer with the material.

Once both shoes were padded, Kalia wriggled a foot into one. The fit wasn't perfect, but the loafer stayed on.

After a few last-minute checks, Kalia looked over to Hasana. She quietly paced over, carefully knelt down and placed a hand on Hasana's shoulder.

"Thank you, my friend," whispered Kalia.

Kalia packed a spare blanket then crept downstairs into the kitchen. After refilling her water skin and grabbing as much spare food as her backpack could carry, she fetched up some Pitacha bread, slathered it with goat butter and emerged from her front door, eating her breakfast on the go.

Having memorised how she had got home from the street where she had jumped off the truck yesterday, Kalia darted away, albeit with a limp, as the morning sun rose up over the rooftops and brought light to the streets.

\*

Hasana glared at the dirt as she power walked down a street towards the fields. She huffed as she turned into an alleyway for a shortcut. She was halfway through to the next street when someone grabbed her by the collar. Hasana yelped as she was pulled into darkness and heard the *clump* of a door closing. A struck match lit an oil lantern. The lantern flame intensified to reveal three masked figures, all with swords. The forth figure, unseen and the one who had dragged Hasana inside, forced her into a chair.

"You are Kalia's friend, yes?" asked a masked man, a ruby on his forehead.

Hasana nodded. Her body tensed as her hands dug into the chair.

The Leader leaned forwards until he was face to face with Hasana. "We need to know where she's going."

\*

Kalia found the street without hassle. Hardly anyone was out at that time of the morning and those that were paid her little attention.

Kalia pictured the steam truck's direction in her head and walked with intent westwards. She stopped when she reached a T-junction.

Kalia exhaled in frustration and glanced down at the ground. A set of tyre tracks in the dirt road continued west. A smile crept upon Kalia's face as she followed the trail.

The road went on for half a mile before Kalia spotted the familiar steam truck. As she approached it, she noticed two men loading the truck with munitions. Upon closer inspection, she flinched. Both men were reanimations, each with a tunnel through their chest and horribly cauterised wounds.

Kalia wondered if she could sneak into the back whilst the slaves worked. She waited for an opening, casually strolled up to the trucks cargo hold, then climbed inside.

Kalia scooted behind a crate to hide from sight. As she snuggled up into her little corner, she questioned how easy it had been to stow away for the third time on the same truck within two days.

"You there, did you spot anyone climbing aboard this vehicle?" came an authoritarian voice.

*"Oh, fumtucks…"* Kalia thought out loud in her head.

The voice that responded was lifeless and monotone. "I have not seen anyone."

There was a brief pause.

"Very good. Return to your hovel in the warehouse. Dahnsee! Come on, we can make good time if we leave now."

Kalia could hear the click and *shlip* of a door opening followed by a few more clicks. A chugging roar brought the truck to life. Shortly afterwards the vehicle doors slammed shut and the steam truck pulled away.

*

Hours later, the smell of vulgar chemicals polluted the air. *"Smells like I've arrived."*

Kalia stirred from her corner and moved towards the curtains. She pulled back the cover to peek at her surroundings, definitely Paghanti village, and waited for the truck to slow down. When it did, she dropped out of the cargo hold and onto the street, stumbling from the shift in motion. She then turned her attention to the Baltuum Mountains before dashing into the nearest alleyway.

On her way to the steep hill path, Kalia drank from her waterskin.

At the edge of the village she hid behind one of the shacks, ensuring no one was within sight, and pulled off her robe.

Kalia kept hold of the gown whilst she ascended the hill, but when she reached the mountainside she bundled it up and stuffed it underneath a rock the size of her head.

Kalia interlocked her fingers and stretched them out in front of her. A chorus of clicks followed. Reaching up to grab a holding, she once again scaled the wall of pocked, smooth rock. Her injuries from the day before made the use of her right arm strenuous, but not unbearable.

The air smelled cleaner as she progressed upwards.

Kalia was surprised when she reached the narrow ledge leading around the mountain. Last time it had felt like an age before she found it. Wearing the loafers felt leagues more reassuring as she found it easier to make purchase upon the craggy surface.

Kalia hugged the wall and shuffled sideways, moving with confident, quick strides.

She finally reached the site where she had plummeted, almost to her demise. Kalia frowned, holding back her shame. The corroding climbing spikes still remained. She slumped down to rest her weary joints for a few minutes before fishing inside her bag for a coil of rope. She thought about tying up to a different spike this time, but both looked secure enough; neither gave any advantage to what Kalia was about to do. She secured the rope to the spike same as before, pulling tight on the knot to ensure it wouldn't slip again. After fastening the rope around her waist like a belt, she faced her destination; the other side of the chasm. Her eyes focused straight ahead, she daren't look down again.

Squeezing her climbing picks, Kalia backed up to get as much of a running start as the ledge would allow.

Bursting into a sprint, she jumped. A sneer of conviction crossed her face as she sailed over the abyss

\*

Four cloaked figures arrived on the outskirts of Paghanti village on the backs of filjinahs, a Suveerian breed of horse with muscular legs, thin grey hair and skin, and heads adorned with three stubby horns. The Leader stopped and surveyed the area. His head moved mechanically, like a cross between an owl and the hands of a clock.

The four rode their beasts through the village. The inhabitants averted their gazes from the newcomers; some expressions tightened in discomfort.

\*

There was no error in Kalia's jump this time. Her picks were held behind her head, ready to strike the rock. Halfway across, her feet sank below the level of the ledge she was aiming for, but her momentum carried her forward. The ledge came up to her neckline. She swung her picks and braced herself.

The crack of mythril on stone and the clomp of her shoes landing on the mountainside echoed. Kalia's climbing picks hooked onto the ledge but were not secure. Her right arm burned and the shock of not falling to her death set in as she gasped for breath. Bringing her focus under control, she struggled to pull herself up. Her left arm clung over the ridge then her head and right arm followed. With a heave of exertion, she drew her body weight up and rolled over.

Kalia lay on her back and let out a chuckle, blinking back a few tears. She sat up and looked across from where she had jumped. She remembered her grandfather's mention of creating a rope bridge. Kalia untied the rope around her waist before finding another spike to tie up. Once finished, the rope stretched across between the two mountains. It wasn't what she thought her grandfather had created, but it gave a much easier means of getting back.

As Kalia traversed the second mountain path, her stomach bubbled and growled. She sighed and slowly crouched down to have a break. There was enough rice left in her skin for a decent meal and it was still moist. She scooped up a generous helping and scoffed a mouthful. The rice still had a mixture of aromatic flavours and tasted just as good as the day it has been made. After another serving, she sealed up the bag. There was still enough for another meal.

The ridge curved upwards, just as her grandfather had written. In the distant sky she spotted circling Baltuum buzzards. Seconds later, the circle descended upon something behind one of the peaks. Despite this unsettling sight, Kalia had a calm, stress-free journey to the next crossing. The cool mountain air bolstered her step. A single bronze rock spike stuck out of the ground to mark the crossing point. Kalia fastened another one of her ropes to the spike and looked down to her next landing spot. The jump would be short, but the landing ledge was further down.

Kalia prepared her mythril picks for good measure. As she steadied her foot against the precipice, it gave way. Her foot slipped as a chunk of rock came loose and fell. She saved herself by quickly turning sideways and latching onto the side. Her skin prickled with self-embarrassment as she climbed back up. Following one last check of her equipment, she jumped.

Pain shot through Kalia's right leg as she landed on the third mountainside path. She screwed up her face and yelled. For the second time in her life she cursed, loudly.

Kalia shrugged off the discomfort and fought onward. The path spanned out, allowing more room for her to stretch. Kalia realised she had travelled further along the route than she had read about in her grandfather's journal.

Reclining against the outcrop, she pulled out the journal and picked up where she had left off.

*It was nice to finally walk along a track that accommodated all three of us, side by side. Further along the path of the third mountain, we found our first cave. Anwar suggested storing our belongings there, but I noticed clumps of fur dotted around the entrance. It was a mountain wolf den. Not wanting to disturb a pack of predators, we pushed onwards.*

*"Wait, am I not on..."* Kalia scanned the path she was on, a tightness in her chest. She continued reading but listened carefully.

*The trail became steep, to the point of having to climb. We were thousands of feet in the air, the abyss below us was black, even in the daylight. The fourth mountain loomed into view. Crossing this divide wasn't an issue, though the barking we heard in the distance didn't set our minds at ease.*

That was all she needed to read. Knowing the opposing mountain was her destination, Kalia packed up the journal and moved with more spring in her step.

A cave mouth appeared in the rock; the smell of old dog wafted from it. Kalia slowed down to tip-toe past the entrance. No sign of any wolves, but plenty of fur tufts scattered along the ground.

The road past the den grew steep and jutted with loose gravel. Kalia had to climb on all fours to scale it.

The sun crawled closer to the horizon. Kalia speculated on sleeping arrangements, hoping to find an empty cave in the fourth mountain.

The final divide approached. It wasn't as wide as the first crossing, but broader than the second.

Kalia checked her rucksack. One coil of rope remained. She sipped from the water skin, replaced it, then prepared for the jump.

With the last cable secured from her waist to the spike, Kalia clasped her climbing picks and leapt across.

The jump was performed well, but the landing ended badly. The edge slammed into Kalia's chest, knocking the wind from her lungs. She whimpered from the impact and her face crumpled in pain as she drew herself up, over and on to safe ground.

Kalia lay on her back again, clutching her chest and wheezing. A dull ringing echoed in her ears. Once she had caught her breath, she sat upright, tied off the rope and brought out the journal for advice on where to go from there.

*Navigating the fourth mountain trail eastwards, the first cave we found was where we settled for dinner. After a hearty meal of beans, we used our flint and tin to set light to our torches and made a start on exploring the cave. The mouth of the cave led into a chamber with three tunnels leading to the north, east and west. I set out to explore the east path, Anwar the north and Uwais the west. My path led to another chamber, almost the same as the first, save for a date written on the wall between the north and east tunnels (D254/Y490, before the Era of Invention). I decided to go east once more and ended up in another room; same design as the last two, except the date on the wall read D300/Y490. I took the east tunnel one more time and came to a dead end with a flat wall. Built into this wall were three stone reels and a gold lever. On the reels were patterns. It took me a moment to realise they were segmented birth emblem designs. The reels moved freely with no stiffness or struggle and as I turned each one, I recognised one of the design parts; my own. I matched each reel until my own birth emblem stared back at me then turned the lever to the right. I heard the sound of shifting stone and the wall moved away to reveal what I had been looking for: a vault.*

With the daylight waning, Kalia tidied away the book and peered into the dingy mouth of the cave. She smiled, excited by the potential treasure within the vault.

Lying on the floor to her left, inside the entrance, was a discarded torch. A fresh stench of pitch could be smelt from where Kalia stood. She searched her backpack for the flint and tin set. Once found, Kalia struck the flint against the tin bar, sending sparks onto the torch. It took many attempts and Kalia grunted in frustration each time, but finally the sparks caught and the torch set ablaze. Picking it up with haste, she held the torch aloft and walked into the bleak, stale atmosphere of the cave.

*

A mass of greyish blue fur bounded out of the den, frantically sniffing the air. Its snout hovered over the wide track in front of it. An unfamiliar scent made its ears prick up; something different and foreign, yet familiar in a way it couldn't recall.

It followed the smell up a steep path; its hooked claws allowing easy travel along awkward terrain. It stopped short of a ridge leading to another mountain and stared towards it.

With the evening sun colouring the sky in orange and purple shades, the creature sat on its hind quarters, raised its head and howled in low foreboding tones.

Human prey was on the mountain.

*

Stalagmites and stalactites dotted the interior of the cave. The colour of the rock walls changed from whitish-grey to light brown.

Kalia surveyed the tunnels. Her torch offered visibility of up to two metres. She reached the room with the three exits going north, east and west. As her grandfather described in his journal, she strolled down the east tunnel.

The shaft narrowed, twisted and turned as Kalia moved onwards. At the next junction room, she turned right again, shining the torch between the north and east tunnels to see the date inscribed on the wall. D254/Y490. The date reassured Kalia's direction.

The second shaft followed the same confusing and claustrophobic pattern as the last. The air grew stale and smelt of filthy stone.

Kalia arrived in the third chamber. Everything looked maddeningly identical to the other two chambers. A glance over the north-east wall revealed the date: D300/Y490.

Kalia travelled down the east tunnel one last time. Knowing the vault was mere moments away, she hastened her step. The burrow smoothed out; the spires of rock were gradually replaced with smoothed, rippled stone. It was like walking through the throat of a grand beast, minus the smell and threat of impending intestinal digestion.

Kalia hit a dead end; a flat surface with three stone reels and an upright, rusted gold lever built into it. Each reel had segments of what looked like bold abstract doodles; birth emblems. She rolled down the first reel until it matched the right third of her birth emblem. After matching the last two reels, she pushed the lever.

A low rumble followed by a *clomp* echoed in the tunnel. The wall moved back and slid sideways.

Kalia stared, dumbfounded, as the vault revealed its contents to her.

*

The Leader stood silently at the top of a steep hill leading to the base of a vast mountain. He scanned the area, head moving in an autonomous manner. Motion, stop, motion, stop.

The other disciples were searching elsewhere for clues. They had to be quick, as the night was fast approaching.

The Leader's eye caught sight of a pale green item of clothing hidden underneath a rock. He strode over and pulled the garment out from under the stone.

Clutching the robe in one hand, he cocked his head to examine it.

The Leader waited patiently for his disciples to return.

*

Kalia entered the vault with caution, slowly moving the torch from side to side and staying on high alert. She spotted an empty sconce on the east wall and rested the torch there. The room was much smaller than she had imagined. Lined up on top of a small shrine along the west wall was what Kalia had been searching for. Two small statues made of gold, a silver necklace set with a sapphire pendant, a strange miniature idol coated in obsidian and a small wooden box.

A large portrait framed in gold and covered in cobwebs caught Kalia's eye. It was of a woman dressed in the finest silk robes,

50

painted in such intricate detail they glimmered through the paintwork and the dust that covered the portrait.

Kalia was mesmerised by the woman's gaze. It was kind, yet commanded respect. She couldn't maintain eye contact with the painting, something about it reminded her of a recent loss and caused her to look away. *"Keep it together, remember what you came for,"* she reminded herself.

Kalia pilfered the trinkets and gilded effigies, shoving them into her rucksack. The shrine was dedicated to Jubael, the god of order; dressed in a toga, he had six arms holding a bowl in each hand and wore a face mask with two sides. Kalia had heard that many prayed to this god during times of war.

She lifted the little wooden box; there were no markings or patterns covering the surface, but it was thick and sturdy. She took a peek inside. A light gleaming gave shape to a thick gold medallion inscribed with an odd language Kalia didn't recognise. A pair of featureless eyes carved in its centre stared back at her. Kalia snapped the box shut and moved it to the bottom of her backpack.

Satisfied with her gains, Kalia picked up the torch and left the vault. As she passed the doorway, a low rumble echoed through the cave and the door resealed itself.

Kalia walked with a new-found energy. Her very first treasure hunt had been a success and for a moment she forgot about the fatigue and aches that held her back.

Retracing her footsteps was no issue and upon reaching the mouth of the cave, Kalia saw that the sky had already turned dark.

*"Guess I'm spending the night here…"*

Kalia propped the torch up against the wall. Its flames were now weak embers, soon to die out. She searched the bag's contents and drew out her blanket, folding it up into a makeshift bed and placing the backpack at the head for use as a pillow. Before lying down to sleep, Kalia picked out her grandfather's journal. The torch's dying fires gave enough light to read by, for now.

*The space was diminutive but perfect for my friends and I to store our investments. On the north wall was a portrait of a woman dressed in fine, glinting garments. I looked closer and was shocked to find that the woman was in fact Queen Fatillarasa.*

Kalia blinked twice at this revelation, she read on with a boost of vigour.

*All paintings and drawings of the ancient Queen were thought to be burned or destroyed after her assassination, all except this one. It could be worth priceless sums of money; alas, it was too big and fragile to take back with us. And yet, my palms were sweating, knowing I had discovered such a rare item.*
*I placed my treasures on top of a miniature shrine along the west wall. It seemed the Queen prayed to the god of order often; a fact I find tragically fitting in hindsight.*
*After placing my items, I retraced my footsteps back to the first room where my comrades were sitting. Uwais told me how his tunnel led him through twists and turns that lead to branching paths, which in turn led to more paths the same. He humbly mentioned how he had collapsed onto his knees and thanked the gods when he got back to the main chamber. Anwar's path had stretched for half a mile before the stench of flammable gases and rot had turned him back.*
*I smiled and directed them down the path I had taken earlier. The door had closed by itself when we returned and the wheels had been changed. Despite my confusion, I showed my friends how to open the chamber door and place their goods inside.*

The light from the torch died out. Kalia fumbled for her bookmark in the darkness, found it, closed the journal and drifted into sleep within seconds.

\*

When Kalia awoke, she strained to get up, but her joints didn't ache as much. She calmly exhaled, knowing she was getting better.

Glancing outside, Kalia saw the dim early morning light through tired eyes. She sat up on her blanket and fetched a roll of Pitacha bread. Kalia forced down the dry, tasteless morsel, longing for a sliver of butter to go with it. After a filling but bland breakfast, she packed up her bedding and walked to the cave exit, leaving the torch behind.

A cool gust of air brushed Kalia's cheek, making her shiver. She had never known temperatures this cold.

Kalia gazed across the mountains and stretched her limbs. The first crossing lay a few hundred yards away.

When she reached the crevasse, the rope Kalia had tied up yesterday remained stretched across it. She unfastened the rope her end and tightened it around her waist, giving the cable a few tugs for reassurance.

Kalia sat on the ledge, held on tight and pushed herself off. She swung towards the other side and her feet landed on the smooth rock face. From there, she had to walk up the wall whilst pulling herself up with the rope. It was far more strenuous than she had anticipated; her body trembled with the fear of falling again.

Finally, Kalia reached the ledge, pulled herself up and rolled onto the pathway. It occurred to her that she was on the mountain with the wolf den, and although the torch would have come in handy, the pitch had already burnt off. Kalia glanced back at the chasm *"No turning back. Hopefully I won't find one…"*

The route widened and Kalia slowed her pace, peeking ahead as she moved. The den came into sight. No sign of life. Kalia trod carefully onwards past the den, her mythril picks drawn like twin swords.

A pebble clinked upon the ground by her feet. Kalia glanced up…

…and gazed into two teal-emerald eyes.

The mountain wolf bared it fangs and leapt down.

Kalia burst into a sprint. The wolf pounced down to where Kalia had been standing, missing her by inches. Fear-induced adrenaline powered Kalia's frantic run down the path to the next crossing. Her breathing was rapid and her eyes stayed open and focused; she never looked behind for fear of slowing down. Yet the wolf was gaining on her, snapping at her heels.

Kalia felt sharp fangs sink into her leg and fell to the ground, screaming. The wolf shook its head violently; Kalia's flesh clenched between its teeth.

The pain was excruciating. Instinctively, she twisted her body around and swung her climbing pick down on its head. The tough mythril metal penetrated the wolf's skull. It yelped and its grip weakened, but still it clung on. Kalia struck again as blood spouted out of the wolf's cranium. Over and over again she stabbed until finally the wolf went limp.

Kalia rose to her feet. Crimson stains streaked across her shredded trouser leg. She tore away at the fabric to get a better look at the damage and winced when she saw the multiple red teeth marks in her calf muscle, leaking blood. She looked at the predator; it was larger than any dog she had ever seen. Hooked claws protruded from lithe but muscular paws. It wore a coat of thick, bluish-grey fur with a mane of jagged, white tipped hair. Far in the distance, a flock of Baltuum buzzards looked on with hungry interest.

Kalia limped to the end of the path where the second rope still dangled from the higher ledge. She locked out the pain as best she could, focused and leapt towards the rope, grabbing it mid-flight. The impact on her legs as she landed on the rock wall sent new signals of pain through her body. She growled and climbed, but her grip grew weak.

Kalia had almost reached the ledge when a hand shot down and grabbed her by the wrist. She screamed until the bearded face of the Sherpa appeared above her.

The Sherpa pulled Kalia up. She embraced him tightly, her terror replaced with relief.

"What are you doing here? How did you find me?" she asked.

"So many questions," he said with a smile. "First, let us clean your wound."

The Sherpa detached a bottle from a patchwork utility belt, made with a mixture of cheap fabric, leather and fine needle work. Among other pouches, a sheathed sabre clung to the belt. He soaked a rag in the bottle's solution and applied it to Kalia's leg. She yelled and sucked air through her teeth; the disinfectant stung like acid.

The Sherpa spoke. "I take strolls through the mountain every day. I spotted you climbing yesterday. However, that's not the reason I came up here. Four men in gold masks are looking for you."

"W-Why me? I don't know anyone who wears a gold mask."

"And I should hope not, but they have swords and a drawing of your birth emblem. Come, we must leave these mountains."

The Sherpa finished cleaning Kalia's wound and applied a bandage using a cloth rag. Thankfully, the bite mark wasn't too deep.

Kalia got to her feet, untied her rope and followed the Sherpa. She relaxed, but bit her lip with stern brows when she realised something.

"Won't the men with masks be waiting for us at the bottom?" she asked.

"Possibly, but there is another route we can take that leads to my home. It will take longer, but hopefully they will not spot us."

Kalia and the Sherpa reached the final crossing, where Kalia's cable was still tautly stretched across the chasm.

"Your mountaineering skills are impressive, but what made you come back here?" he asked.

Kalia felt numb again and let out a heavy sigh. "Remember how you told me to think about my parents the next time I tried this?"

The Sherpa nodded.

Kalia continued. "I'm trying my best not to, now that they're gone." Her voice broke as she finished.

The Sherpa looked away, shaking his head slowly. "I am sorry, my words were only meant to deter you." He knelt down to check the tightness of the rope. "I used to work the cocoa fields when I was young. I wanted to be free of that lifestyle more than anything. When I was old enough to leave, I didn't give it a second thought. Living off the land and in poverty was far better."

The Sherpa motioned Kalia to cross first. She grabbed the rope tightly, hooked both legs around, hung upside down and monkey-crawled across. This method was uncomfortable as the course fibres rubbed up against Kalia's wolf bites. She winced and grunted all the way along.

The tightrope held fast and she reached the other side, awkwardly clambering up onto the mantle.

Once Kalia was safely across, the Sherpa untied the rope at his end and tightened it around his waist; swinging his way across and climbing up without hassle.

The Sherpa pointed down the track. "See how the path continues further right? We need to travel that way. The route will keep us out of sight, but will be steeper and trickier to traverse."

Kalia nodded and let the Sherpa lead the way. True to his warning, the ridge narrowed quickly until there was nothing but rough foundation. They would have to navigate a vertical surface.

Kalia noticed a pair of bronze climbing picks attached to the Sherpa's belt, both coated in a fine layer of powdered stone. He equipped himself with both, dug them into the cliff face and climbed sideways in a crablike fashion. Kalia watched his movements carefully then followed suit, her mythril tippers easily penetrating the rock.

The Sherpa called out, "There's a sill we can rest on further ahead. I hope you have some rations remaining."

Kalia's arms grew tired; she had been scrabbling for nearly a quarter of an hour and the strain on her body was exhausting. The Suveerian heat only made matters worse. Every time Kalia found footing on a tiny outcrop, she stretched and rested her arms. But these outcrops were not found often and the Sherpa didn't wait for Kalia to catch up.

Finally, she spotted a flat track beyond.

When they made it, the Sherpa touched down first then reached out to help Kalia. She collapsed when her feet found stable ground.

"We should rest for a while. We have managed the worst part of the journey, but still have a way to go to reach my cabin."

Kalia fished around in her backpack for food. Only half a roll of Pitacha bread along with her rice and water skins remained. She opted for the rice, as it had to be three days old by now. The rice had turned sour, but Kalia ate it regardless. The final meal her mother had given her was finished.

The Sherpa gazed out across the peaks whilst chewing on a piece of bread. Once finished, he stood up without a word.

"Are you well rested?"

Kalia rotated her shoulder. "Yes, I'm ready."

*

Kalia and the Sherpa continued their journey around the mountainside, rock towering over them. The wind died down and the heat rose. A segment of sky appeared between two cliffs. Kalia traipsed on with determination, knowing she would finally arrive on level ground.

The mantle stooped down into a steep, pebble strewn incline. The Sherpa turned around and descended backwards, his picks spraying dust clouds and sending stones tumbling down with every strike. Kalia followed on in the same manner. The distance between the mountains narrowed.

Excited, Kalia moved too quickly and the Sherpa called up to tell her to slow down.

Finally, the Sherpa touched down at the base. Kalia jumped down and fell to her hands and knees, grateful to be on a surface she couldn't fall from. She was on a narrow path and above her the sky was a small, thin streak of blue that opened up further ahead, like a river spanning out into an ocean.

Kalia glanced eastwards.

"Down that path, is that where you found me before?" she asked.

"Yes, it leads to the pit you landed in. The walls there are too solid and curved to climb. Come, my home is not far now."

Their passage curved and was caked with dirt and rubble.

After what felt like an hour's walk, the mountains that surrounded them opened up, revealing the landscape of the Galhadeen region. Farms, small settlements and fields stretched out as far as the eye could see. The Sherpa didn't stop to admire the views but walked on, northwest bound. In the distance, Kalia could see the Sherpa's ramshackle cabin.

As they approached the shack, the Sherpa stopped suddenly, his hand splayed behind him to stop Kalia.

"Wait here," he said.

"What's wrong?" Kalia asked, her eyes moving from the cabin to the Sherpa.

The Sherpa's face betrayed his calm response. "I won't be a second. Just need to check if my home is tidy."

The Sherpa paced towards his front door, a hand upon his scabbard. He took cover by the door, his other hand slowly reaching for the wooden latch.

The Sherpa turned the handle and pushed the door open.

Kalia spotted someone creeping inside the shaded room.

"Look out!" she shouted.

The Sherpa drew his sword. Whoever was inside drew their weapon and backed up into a crouch.

Before the Sherpa could call out, he heard the thump of footsteps. He moved out of the way as an oil-sheened blade shot through the wall, but not before it sliced his eye. The Sherpa stumbled, grunted and covered the bleeding side of his face. Kalia raised her hands to her mouth. A figure stomped out of the house. He wore a gold mask and a grey, hooded robe. The tip of his polished backsword dripped with blood.

The Sherpa raised his sabre to parry a downward chop.

"Kalia! Run!" the Sherpa yelled.

The masked man and the Sherpa exchanged swipes, strikes and parries. The Sherpa fought with controlled aggression. The masked man moved with grace.

Kalia stood, fear stricken.

"I said run!" yelled the Sherpa.

*"No!"* Kalia's fear turned into a rage filled snarl.

She scanned the ground around her and found a thick rock with smooth features. She lifted the rock and hurled it towards the assassin.

The rock missed the assailant, landing with a thump at his feet. It had the intended effect. The masked man flinched for a mere second. The distraction allowed the Sherpa to cut a swath along the assassin's chest. Another swipe across the man's neck sent a splash of blood across the dusty ground.

Kalia trembled at the sight, her jaw slack. The Sherpa sheathed his blade and marched over to Kalia. He grabbed her by the shoulders and shook her.

"I told you to run," he scolded.

Kalia snapped out of her shock. "I'm not leaving! I've lost everyone, I-I'm not losing you too!" Kalia welled up again, her voice wavering.

The Sherpa took his hands away and sighed. "Forgive me, I wasn't thinking straight. Letting you run away would have lead you right into their hands."

"Who are they?"

"I do not know. Regardless, we have been found. I need to get you to the nearest settlement, ahk…"

The Sherpa cupped a hand over his left eye. He fumbled for his bottle of disinfectant. Tilting his head back he unscrewed the tin cap and poured a splash into his damaged eye socket. He gritted his teeth and grunted in pain as the alkali cleaned the wound.

The Sherpa searched around the side of his cabin. He beckoned Kalia close when he saw something. Kalia rounded the corner and saw a filjinah. It fidgeted at the sight of the two unfamiliar humans.

"Hmm, he will not be needing that anymore," said the Sherpa to himself as he glanced over at the assassin's corpse. He turned to Kalia. "Do you require any supplies before we leave?"

"Yes please, any food or water you can spare would help."

The Sherpa led Kalia inside the cabin. Although he had barely any food to spare, Kalia managed to refill her waterskin.

Once outside, the Sherpa cautiously approached the filjinah and untied its reigns. It made no sudden movements. The Sherpa mounted the saddle first then helped Kalia up behind him. With a flick of the reigns and a shout of "Jeya!" the filjinah shot forwards so quickly that Kalia almost barrelled off the backend. She gripped the Sherpa's waist tightly as they rode onwards to a settlement in the distance.

*

In the shadow of a hill, the Leader lowered his spyglass and stored it away in his filjinah's saddlebag.

*

Kalia and the Sherpa finally reached a small village known as Wakanashil, far west-southwest of Paghanti village. Kalia knew what it was like to live in poverty but not on this scale.

Every house was ramshackled; hastily put together and missing vital elements, including doors. The putrid stench of decay and human waste roamed beyond the village boarders. Kalia had assumed it was the filjinahs until they entered the settlement and the smell grew to a nauseating foulness.

They trotted down the main road but didn't find any pleasant sights. Flies spun over holes in the ground next to buildings, where people dumped everything, including what they had digested. Rats scampered freely across the street without fear. Stick-thin beggars sprawled alongside the main road wearing nothing but loin cloths and raised their frail hands pleadingly for anything the two could spare.

The Sherpa tied the filjinah to a post and water trowel that contained nothing but dried muck.

As evening darkened the sky, Kalia dreaded the idea of resting here for the night. The locals that weren't slumped on the streets either looked at her with dull curiosity or ignored her altogether.

"I am sorry, but we will never reach Galhadeen by nightfall. We will need to rest here for the night," said the Sherpa.

"But where will we rest? The people here look like they don't have beds to sleep on," Kalia replied.

"I know of someone who can offer us shelter."

They walked away from the main road and down fetter-smeared alleyways. At least the waste pits weren't dug in down the passageways. They reached a shack that appeared to have some degree of effort put into its design. It was long, with one wall made of stacked stones whilst the other partitions were built with a mixture of wood and duststone. A corner of the hay-thatched roof was black from being scorched and burned away. Holes pocked its canvas.

The Sherpa opened the rickety door and Kalia followed behind. Inside, a middle-aged woman sat on a tiny stool smoking from an old pooshka; a charcoal pipe adorned with gilded designs and friezes that had long since worn away. It took the woman a moment to recognise the Sherpa.

"Ah, Balshadee! What happened to your eye?"

Kalia's ears pricked up, surprised to hear the Sherpa's name at last. Balshadee waved off the question. "It's nothing to worry about, Mikina. I am in need of a bed for the night. How are your rates?"

"For you, only the best," said Mikina with a toothless smile. "One hundred iritons."

Balshadee winced at the price. "I might struggle with that rate."

Mikina waved her hand dismissively. "Then crekk off and go elsewhere... ha, just kidding. What have you got?"

"Hold on," Kalia interjected. She rummaged around in her backpack and pulled out a silver necklace; one of the trinkets from the vault room she had pilfered.

Mikina scrutinised the item. She smiled and nodded. "Ah, yes, very nice." Her face turned into a scowl. "What use would I have for this?"

"Err, wait, hold on." Kalia scrabbled inside her rucksack for the money she had earned from working the coffee fields, pulling out a bag and counting the coins inside. "I have sixty iritons saved up."

Mikina dragged on her pooshka and chewed it over in her mind. After exhaling a plume of dry, choking, tobacco tainted smoke, she answered. "Hmm, you are a hardworking girl no? Ok, for sixty iritons you can stay here."

Kalia handed over the money bag. "Thank you."

Mikina smiled and pointed to a hay pile in the corner. "You are welcome. Your bed is over there."

"And what about my friend?" asked Kalia.

"That will be another one hundred iritons."

Before Kalia could protest, Balshadee stepped in. "It's fine, I will rest outside and keep watch."

"I'm not tired. May I join you for a bit?" Kalia asked.

"Of course."

"I will have your bed ready for you later, see you then," said Mikina, who went back to smoking her pooshka and gazing off at nothing.

Kalia and Balshadee left the inn and spotted a small hill a few yards behind the shack. They hunched down on the hillside and Kalia sipped from her water skin. The stench had subsided but still lingered, hanging in the back of Kalia's senses and putting her off eating any more for the day.

"So what made you become a Sherpa?" asked Kalia.

Balshadee gazed up at the stars. "I keep telling myself it is for the freedom of the surrounding mountains. But in truth, it is because I am a coward."

"That can't be true, you've saved my life more times than I can repay."

Balshadee gave a small smile. "For women it is mostly voluntary to join the militia but men are called into service when they reach a certain age. Rather than fight for this country, I fled, away from my family and my home." Balshadee breathed deeply and sighed. "And I didn't stop running until I came to the Baltuum Mountains. I stole food and water before I began hunting local wildlife. You would be surprised how tasty roasted quadrugorge spiders are."

Kalia shuddered. "I can only guess."

"My point is, I had a choice: fight and die or live a pitiful existence."

"It's not pitiful. You're wise, you've built your own home, you know the mountains like the back of your hand and you're a great swordsman."

Balshadee's smile broadened but sadness still clouded his eyes. "And you are too kind."

Kalia smiled back and they both relaxed into silence.

After a few minutes Kalia leaned over and hugged the Sherpa, wishing him goodnight before heading off to bed.

Inside the inn Mikina, was half asleep, propped up on the stool and mumbling incoherently.

A thin layer of cloth covered the hay pile and Kalia at least had a candle to read with. She lit it using the flame from a rusting oil lamp in the corner next to Mikina.

Kalia placed the candle behind the bed and eased herself down. The hay was supportive but stray strands poked through the cloth, irritating her skin. She read from her grandfather's journal one more time.

*The journey back was simple in practice. We used the ropes we had tied off to climb over the chasms. But for one of us, the journey came to a tragic end.*
*We had just passed the wolf den when we heard a growl. We ran but Anwar was pounced upon by a Baltuum wolf. During the*

*struggle, both Anwar and the wolf tumbled over the edge. Anwar screamed all the way down. The rest of the journey back was accompanied with an uncomfortable silence. Uwais refused to talk. When we finally returned to Paghanti village, we held a small prayer for our lost friend. Uwais severed contact with me days later. Much like myself, he grieves. The journey dashed his sense of adventure.*

.

The chapter ended there.

Kalia browsed the contents on the first page and read a quick report on the quadrugorge spider, also known as the horse eating spider. She closed the book after reading a paragraph and shuddered. She blew out the candle and fell asleep.

*

Kalia awoke with a start. She could hear shouting outside. Mikina still sat slumped against the stone-cobbled wall in a semi-comatose state.

Kalia heard Balshadee cry out over the sound of clashing metal from outside.

"Kalia, run!"

Kalia fetched up her backpack but realised she had nowhere to run. She looked around to see moonlight creeping through an opening in the inn's wood panelling. She checked the stability, found its fittings to be poorly fastened and kicked hard at the plank.

The door burst open and a cloaked figure walked in; a segment of his gold mask reflected in the oil lamp's glow. Kalia didn't stop to stare, but frantically kicked harder. The wood snapped and broke off. The figure loomed closer and drew his sword.

Before the shadowed man could reach her, he turned around and swung his sword at a stool flying towards him. The movement was quick and frightening. Two lumps of wood parted either side of him.

Mikina stood defiantly, hand outstretched.

"You no pay? You get out, you ruffian scubby!"

Another panel broke. Kalia pushed her rucksack through first then crawled outside after it. *"Where's the filjinah?"* Kalia darted through the alleyways towards the main road. She tripped over littered pots and bumped into walls on the way, the pitch-black back-streets difficult to navigate despite the moon in the sky.

Kalia reached an alleyway and managed to spot a wide-open space at the end of it. She burst through the alley and onto the main road, where the filjinah was tied up. Sheer luck prevented her from tumbling into the waste pits.

Kalia sprinted over to the horse and worked to undo the knots. She had the filjinah untied before another cloaked figure appeared on the main road.

Kalia jumped up onto the beast's back but she slipped and her seating position was askew, hanging off the side of the beast.

Grabbing the reins in one hand and yelling "Jeya!" she sped off down the dirt road, clinging on tightly.

Eventually, Kalia adjusted herself to sit upright, not helped by the bouncing gallop. Adrenaline fuelled her sleep-deprived head.

The village of Wakanashil quickly passed her by and she was out on the barren lands, unsure of where she was going.

*"Think! Galhadeen city is to the west, so just go that way."*

Kalia whipped the reins once more and the filjinah brayed, increasing its pace. Fear prevented Kalia from looking behind her;

only the road ahead mattered, so she kept her sights focused forward.

Kalia's mind started drifting. Her eyelids drooped and her head followed suit. A harsh bump in the ride snapped her awake. Angry at her restless condition, Kalia snarled and willed herself to remain conscious.

Suddenly the filjinah tripped, found its footing again but then slowed down. Its breathing became heavy, it brayed with a stammer and its movements were sluggish. The creature swayed back and forth, its knees shaking violently.

Kalia jumped off the falling beast's heavy frame as it crashed to the ground with a loud fleshy thump, spreading dust clouds out in all directions.

Kalia got her bearings and pushed the filjinah's back, begging it to stand up. The animal remained motionless, stuck in rigid paralysis.

That was when Kalia noticed something on the beast's leg.

Upon closer inspection, she saw that the hoof was covered in a viscous, silky substance that stuck to her fingers. Kalia spotted something else stuck in its flesh; several coarse barbs with lime green secretions.

A noise skittered from behind her. Kalia turned around.

On the ground, at calf height, was a creature of eight, stocky hairy legs, four black pearl eyes and an abdomen covered in barbs. Kalia had seen it before in her grandfather's journal. She tensed up, unable to look away.

The quadrugorge spider darted towards the prone filjinah.

Two other spiders followed it, popping out from the ground with a cloud of dust.

Kalia resisted the urge to scream and cower. She desperately scoured her backpack for a weapon and her hands found the mythril picks. Ignoring the tingle that crawled across her skin, Kalia swung down wildly on the spider covering the filjinah's thigh. The pick's sturdy metal pierced the spider's thorax. The spider squirmed but the other two were devouring her mount's neck and flesh around the ribcage. Kalia turned her attack on them, thrashing wildly as pus-like, cream-coloured fluid splattered everywhere.

By the time all three spiders were dead, the damage had already been done. The filjinah's eyes stared, transfixed in horror, its neck pooling blood.

Kalia strained to keep her frustration in check, withholding a scream. She clenched her only weapons, wiped away the spider blood and began travelling in the direction the filjinah's corpse was facing.

*

Three masked individuals traipsed across the warm landscape. They would have taken their filjinahs, but spotting quadrugorge spider webs was difficult under the cover of night. It didn't matter, their target would not get far.

The Leader cursed silently under his breath.

"What troubles you, my leader?" asked a subordinate.

"A teenage girl managed to escape us. I feel our quest should have ended in Wakanashil and yet we still pursue her," the Leader responded.

"Exhaustion will take her. Then we can take what remains," said the other subordinate.

The Leader didn't reply. His hand twitched around his sword's hilt. *"So many dead, so much time wasted. All thanks to a selfish little girl."*

*

Kalia's legs trembled under her relentless movement. She was tired and no matter which direction she faced, nothing but the reddish-brown dirt of Suveer-Kotol surrounded her. Her grandfather's journal contained a map, but without a sense of direction, she could have been walking in circles, for all she knew.

Kalia's feet were blistered and the sun was encroaching on the skyline. She stopped to grab some food from her rucksack, pulling out a piece of jerky the Sherpa had given her. Her eyes stung. The realisation that Balshadee was dead sunk in.

Kalia dropped to her knees, squeezing the jerky in one hand and clenching the dirt in the other.

*"Give up. Everyone you meet dies."*

"I…" she whispered.

*"Just let them catch you, no one else has to die."*

"I can't…" her voice quivered. She shook her head and let out a sob.

*"Give up. Lie down. Let them win."*

She stared up at the sky through eyes that prickled from tears and fatigue, squeezing the dirt in her hand. She let out a furious roar before taking deep, meditative breaths; gradually calming down.

Kalia chomped down on the jerky and pressed onwards with a sense of angered determination. The land's repetitive form stretched on as far as the eye could see.

By the time the sun broke the borderline, a new piece of natural land structure appeared; a long crack that dropped down into a valley that stretched and curved for miles. Thinking of a potential hiding place and shelter from the sun, Kalia squirmed downwards.

From inside the narrow valley, the sky looked like a bolt of thick lightning. The claustrophobic confines expanded little by little the further she travelled. When the width of the walls grew to two metres, Kalia noticed burrows in the sides of the gorge; one every twenty yards and big enough for a toddler to crawl through. She travelled on, the air much cooler in the shade.

A low, stammering hiss reverberated within the ravine.

Kalia halted and glanced around. She saw nothing and the sound didn't repeat, so she continued her travel.

Something landed behind her.

Kalia spun around and caught a full glimpse of a figure wearing a silver trimmed hooded robe and a gold mask with a ruby encrusted on the forehead. Another two men dropped in behind him; same clothing, sans the ruby on the forehead.

"Give us the medallion," commanded the Leader.

Kalia did not respond. Instead she turned around and ran.

The three cloaks followed in pursuit.

*

A scaled creature, thirty feet long and a foot wide, detected movement from outside its den. It slithered closer to the source, hungry for a meal. But as it drew closer, the creature sensed the presence of three other life forms, a little bigger than the first. With the prospect of a larger meal and some snacks for later, it waited in the darkness, close to the exit of the burrow.

As the group moved into range, the creature lunged out at a frightening speed, sinking its fangs into the nearest victim. The taste of human prey was satisfyingly delicious. It did not have time to enjoy its meal. Its teeth hung on to the prey as its head was severed.

*

Kalia kept running, unaware of her pursuers' disrupted progress.

The enclosed valley followed a zigzag pattern. At the end it widened out tremendously to reveal a crater. In the centre of the crater was a town made up of twisted buildings.

Kalia couldn't spot any inhabitants but slid down the incline towards the settlement.

The colour of the ground changed from reddish-brown to grey and appeared infertile. The sun's rays diminished inside the town's confines, degrading everything of colour and intense heat.

When Kalia reached the town's perimeter, she scanned the warped structures around her; unnatural curves and twists that would be pointless, and impossible, to mould with human hands. The buildings were still made of duststone but stretched and folded in a way the materials wouldn't make possible. Windows and doorframes were unsymmetrical; some looked like the gaping mouths of tortured victims. There were no straight, streamlined streets and every structure was placed in an odd, haphazard position.

As Kalia paced down the curved streets, something stirred in a home to her right. She looked towards it but couldn't make anything out.

Someone shuffled out of an alleyway. Hairless with a featureless face, it was like a layer of skin had been stretched across its eyes and mouth, with its birth emblem distorted across various parts of its face.

Others like it crawled into view.

They spoke in pained whispers that echoed inside Kalia's mind, the same word over and over again.

*"Why?"*

Kalia pretended to ignore them and pressed onwards.

*

The Leader pried the Kabahnsheer serpent's fangs from his comrade's gut. The serpent's head housed many small horns that spread over its curves like hair. The fangs had left large holes that seeped blood out of his comrade's stomach.

"Get to your feet!" the Leader commanded, throwing the serpent's head aside. "We are not finished here."

The injured comrade strained to bring himself to a standing position. He clutched his wounds as he followed his allies. The Leader snarled under his breath.

*

The inhabitants gazed with sightless eyes at Kalia. Treading slowly towards her, the Misshapen moved their heads in confused wonder at the newest arrival.

Kalia's eyes darted around, looking for a place to stop. She needed to see this town on a map just to get an idea of where she was. But of all the times she queried her grandfather about the settlements outside their own city, he had never spoken of a place like this.

The Misshapen wouldn't stop whispering. Kalia winced and covered her ears.

"What do you mean why? What's wrong?" she called out to them.

73

The Misshapen did not respond, save for their repetitive moans of
*"Why?"*

The street curled around a tight corner. More contorted buildings
and misshapen people appeared the further Kalia pushed on. A
gaggle advanced towards her, blocking her progress. The group's
voices echoed over each other, making their droning more intense.
Kalia gritted her teeth, looked for an opening and ran.

The Misshapen reached out to grab her, their movements
quickening when they were close. Kalia ducked under a swipe and
weaved in and out of the nightmares that stalked the streets.

*

Three cloaked men drew their swords as the misshapen nightmares
confined upon them, forcing them into a circle.

"I have no time for this. Press onwards or die here," snarled the
Leader as he cut down the faceless man in front of him and
advanced.

Two of the cloaks made good progress, but the injured one fell
behind and was set upon by a large cluster of the Misshapen. They
moved with surprising speed. Hands of varying sizes hammered
down on the injured one, pummelling his flesh and tearing at his
clothes. From within the melee, a gold, bloodied mask was tossed
aside and landed with a dull thump.

"Leave him!" the Leader ordered as he decapitated another
Misshapen. "I will not wait for you."

*

Kalia passed a building she swore looked like a rubula donut. None
of the structures that sat along the streets made any sense in their
design. The road curved round, but to where, Kalia didn't know.
Her ribs stung from a stitch and she dared not think of the state her

feet might be in by this point. Shadows and more Misshapen appeared the deeper she delved into the town.

Finally, Kalia reached the town centre, the core of the crater.

Two corroded bronze poles topped with a sphere of the same material lay deformed and out of shape, various pieces of teslatronic equipment surrounding them. Symbols were burnt into the ground around the pile and a scent of ozone still hung in the air. Kalia approached the wreckage, mystified by the apparatus.

After a quick examination, she looked around for an exit. The curvature of the streets made her lose direction yet again.

Kalia sighed and picked the path she assumed led north. Scuffled cries of annoyance sounded off in the distance. She pressed on with haste, taking the water skin from her backpack to drink on the go.

More curves, twists and turns awaited Kalia. Her focus remained on a potential exit from the madness that surrounded her. Kalia could see the top of the crater above the rooftops and the sight boosted her momentum.

A pair of arms wrapped themselves around her waist. Kalia yelped and swung her elbows around as she was squeezed and shaken. The right one caught her assailant in the side of the head and they loosened their grip on her, allowing Kalia to squirm out of the aggressive hug. By this point more Misshapen had surrounded her, charging with outstretched arms.

Kalia sprawled onto her knees and crawled, snaking through an open pair of legs as the malformed tumbled over themselves to grab her.

Looking ahead and seeing that the path was mostly clear, she rushed on, darting around those in her way like a lethal game of tag.

A rubble-strewn, steep incline came into view.

The cries of the townsfolk changed from querying whispers to low, chilling moans. The inhabitants stopped taking notice of Kalia and passed her by, shuffling towards the centre of town.

Kalia heaved off her backpack and equipped herself with the climbing picks. *"One last mountain,"* she thought as she gazed up at the summit.

The long, eerie groans grew louder. Kalia looked behind her.

Gaiting towards her was the Leader of the masked men, his cloak stained with blood and his backsword dripping with crimson. His two acquaintances were nowhere to be seen.

Kalia threw her backpack on, and leapt up the cliff face, sinking her picks into it. The soil was softer than the high-density rock of the Baltuum Mountains.

As she climbed, the Leader called out to her.

"Give me the medallion! Why do you continue to run? I can get you out of this country, away from the war!" Gone was the Leader's calm, collected speech; now he spoke with irritation and anger.

Kalia blocked out his bargaining and forced her way up the incline. It was almost vertical and the climbing picks were more for stability than anything else.

The Leader rushed towards the slope as the Misshapen tried to flank him. He reached the base of the wall, sheathed his sword and followed Kalia up before the Misshapen could overwhelm him.

Kalia remained focused on the top, despite her exhaustion and hunger, but her vision was blurring and she was slowing down. Kalia's grip grew weak. Her nerves trembled. Survival didn't seem so important anymore.

A hand clasped her left ankle, snapping her out of her daze. Kalia looked down to see the Leader staring up at her with black, obscured eyes. His hand reached for his scabbard as he hung from Kalia and tried to find purchase on the hillside with his feet.

Rage tightened Kalia's grip on her climbing tools. She held on for dear life as she lowered herself, just close enough to reach the Leader's face, then raised her right foot and sent it down into his face; the loafer's hardened leather sole slamming against the gold mask. The Leader was briefly stunned but drew his sword halfway out. Kalia thrust another two kicks; one to the Leader's fingers and the other to his face. The ruby embedded in the mask came loose and fell to the crowd below. The hand around her leg loosened grip a little. The Leader drew his bloodied backsword. Ignoring the attack, he aimed the blade for a lunge.

Before the Leader could impale Kalia, her foot shot down one more time.

The hand came loose.

The gold-masked man didn't scream as he fell into the sea of Misshapen humans at the bottom and was swallowed by the mob. Fists and arms rained down on him like teeth chewing food.

Kalia didn't look down. Her focus returned to the climb. Her reserves of energy were running on empty. Knowing she could finally rest at the summit pushed her upwards. Every time Kalia felt tired or weary, she lightly head-butted the wall. The pain worked like coffee.

When she reached the top, Kalia rolled up onto the ledge and sprawled out.

She sucked in quick gasps of air and let out stammered cries; a mixture of pain and relief. Once her breathing stabilised, she fell asleep within seconds.

Kalia awoke with a slow, lethargic sigh. Her mouth was dry. She glanced down at herself and smiled, relieved that she hadn't been eaten in her sleep.

Beams of sunlight shone down on her as she pulled herself up to her knees. Judging by the sun's position, it was around noon.

Kalia drank the last dregs from her water skin. She checked her rucksack for food; one piece of jerky and a few crumbs of Pitacha bread. She gobbled them down, then fetched the journal, opening up the back pages where the map of Suveer-Kotol had been drawn. Her finger trailed the map. *"Let's see. There's Wakanashil so this must be... Clibousten?"*

According to the map, Clibousten was close to the sea and east of Galhadeen. If Kalia reached the sea and followed it west, another seaside town would appear before she reached the city. Clibousten, Wakanashil and the seaside town of Nababru bad been hand-drawn onto the map.

Kalia picked up her equipment and walked down the fissure, partially shaded from the sun.

When the fissure narrowed to a metre in width, Kalia climbed out onto the open, red dirt expanse. She turned three-hundred and sixty degrees in the hope of spotting a land mark.

Kalia stopped, took a few steps forward and squinted. A line of deeper blue appeared in the far distance.

Kalia trekked on.

*

The sea was as beautiful as Kalia remembered it. She had seen it once or twice; beautiful cobalt, calm and vast.

She stood on an expansive stretch of beach and smiled. Waves of cool water lapped at her feet, bringing back memories of better times, paddling in the sea. Kalia closed her eyes and breathed in deeply, absorbing the salty wind.

Feeling rejuvenated, Kalia strolled along the beach, heading west. Crabs the size of dogs appeared but minded their own business, picking at the sand with pincers big and strong enough to snap bones.

Miles of walking through the sea-swept, soft sand in bare feet did wonders for Kalia's blisters.

She spotted rooftops on the horizon and began to move with a spring in her step, whilst remaining cautious of jagged rocks and monstrous crabs.

*

Kalia reached the port town of Nababru, made up mostly of sand. Only ten docks in total were built along its half mile-long stretch. Most of the buildings in the area were either run-down or abandoned. Wooden shutters hung snapped or rotten from the windows. Few people roamed the streets and fewer took any notice of Kalia.

Docked in Berth Three was a ship. It was much bigger than a humble merchant vessel; four bronze cannons poking out from the sides surrounded by red painted wooden frames with bronze panelling. Its sails were black and a closer inspection revealed a decal: a skull with one raised eyebrow and a frothing tankard beside it.

*

Three people stood on the dock next to the ship in the middle of a transaction; one Caucasian and two Suveerians. The Caucasian was male with long black hair, a chin stripe beard and a knee-length red coat with gold buttons and lining. A cutlass hilt poked out from underneath his jacket. He signed a few papers and handed them over to the Suveerian dock masters.

A young Suveerian girl appeared at his side. She smiled and spoke to him in a language he couldn't understand. He glanced at her and cleared his throat. An awkward smile spread across his face. He looked around, but the dock masters had already left. One of his crewmates passed him by and he reached out and grabbed his shoulder.

"Hey Winchester. How's your Suveerian?"

Winchester was old, with a well-trimmed handlebar moustache. His linen shirt and braces were tight around the girth of his belly. A revolver sat in a holster around his waist.

"You got communication problems again?" he asked the Captain.

"Yes, this girl wants something."

"She's trying to sell you somethin'," said Winchester, shaking his head.

The little girl spoke up, again in her own language.

Winchester stopped and glanced at the girl, changing from his strange accented Orthodox to passable Suveerian. "We don't often people take." His phrasing wasn't perfect, but he could be understood.

"I can offer something of value," she spoke slowly as she pulled out from her rucksack a silver necklace embedded with a sapphire.

Winchester lifted up the gem segment and examined it with a monocular. After half a minute of close examination, he pulled the Captain aside and whispered to him, their backs turned to the girl. "Okay, so she's looking for safe passage out of this country and wants to pay us with the necklace. It's genuine. Worth about four trips."

The Captain stroked his chin. "Then let's bring her along."

"Where we plannin' on taking her?"

"Sailors' Respite, off the coast of Chivralor, where else?"

"What! Are you forgettin' the navy'll blow us outta the water the moment they see a black flag?"

"As long as we can reach Sailors' Respite without any hassle, it'll be worth it. You said so yourself, that necklace is worth four journeys. Plus Tricky's magic usually keeps us hidden."

Winchester grumbled. "Mer, yeah it's not the riskiest thing we've ever done... yet." He turned to the girl. "We take you Sailors' respite," he said in mangled Suveerian.

Kalia smiled. "Thank you."

"We leave in hour. You either sleep ship or you own thing."

Kalia smirked, one eyebrow bent, withholding laughter from the slap-dash job of Suveerian vocabulary.

"My name is Winchester Wright, my boat is The Procrastination and he, Captain Cortain," Winchester motioned to the Captain who gave a curt bow.

Kalia introduced herself. "If I may, I would like to go for a quick walk. I will be back in an hour. You will receive your pay then." She had to simplify her language to make sure he understood.

Winchester grunted in agreement.

Kalia clasped the necklace and skipped into town.

*

## 'Magical Margaret's Mystical Merchandise'

The shop sign was so bright and colourful that it was hard to miss; gold letters with strokes of purples, greens and blues for a background and a glossy finish. The shop was the only building in the street to have glass windows, small as they were.

A brass bell chimed as Kalia entered. The inside was crowded with all manner of strange items and artefacts. Small statues stood alongside burlap stitched dolls, glass orbs inset with swirling colours sat next to hanging rainbow threaded dream catchers. Smoky incense of opium flavoured the air.

A woman with youthful features but long, wiry, greying hair walked in from a back room. She wore a purple dress lined with gold and silver painted seashell sequins that shimmered as she walked. Her eyes were a hypnotic greyish-blue. Despite her Caucasian appearance, she spoke fluent Suveerian.

"Good evening, little one. Welcome to Magical Margaret's Mystical Merchandise. I have everything from love potions to Ouija boards. Just kidding, I'm sold out of Ouija boards."

"Err... I... hello," Kalia responded, rubbing her arm.

The woman smiled. "Let me try a different greeting. My name is Magical Margaret. How can I help you?"

Kalia stuck her hand into her rucksack as she spoke. "I have something. Can you tell me what it is?"

She pulled out a wooden box and handed it to Margaret, who scrutinised the pure gold medallion inside, holding it up and turning it over. Kalia's face tightened, resisting the desire to protest, her eyes watching Margaret's every move. Margaret placed the medallion back in the box, walked over to the till and put the box on the counter.

"One second," she said as she paced into the back room.

A minute later, Margaret came back with a big, orange, leather bound book with brass corner plates. She flicked through the pages and stopped suddenly on an illustration of an angel. Margaret's head moved with her eyes as she read with stern, frantic speed.

"The medallion is made from a metal known as angel gold or Pietrymus. According to legend, angels existed on Orran before the Savage Era began over five hundred years ago." Margaret pointed to the box. "To the right person, that chunk of metal is priceless. Pietrymus is so rare that its very existence was thought a myth."

Kalia looked down at the box, unsmiling. "But what does it do? My grandfather wanted to keep it safe. People tried to kill me for it."

"If my understanding of astral magic travel is correct, it's a dimensional key. If used with powerful astral magics it can open a portal to Altumeria; the realm of angels. You may be hunted for as long as you hold it. You need to keep it somewhere safe."

"Can I leave it with you?"

Margaret blinked and raised an eyebrow. "You would wish me to be hunted?"

"Wha... no, no I would never. It's just... why can't I just throw it in the sea? Why didn't I just give it to the first person who wanted it?" Kalia became stressed, throwing her arms up and rubbing her eyes.

Margaret remained silent, giving Kalia time to calm down. "If you throw it away, someone else will find it. If you had given it up, someone may have killed you for its location. This kind of artefact can drive men mad with gold lust and, in the wrong hands, can doom this world."

"You said it opens... something to a world of angels? Why would that be a bad thing?"

Margaret looked serious. "Not all angels are good by nature. They can be just as evil as the men on Orran. I'm sorry I couldn't give you any good news."

Kalia said nothing. She nodded and turned to leave.

"Hold on," said Margaret. "If you want, I can read your palm, free of charge."

"What will that do?" Kalia asked.

"By reading your palm, I can foresee your future and look into your past."

Kalia failed to hide her surprise. "You can do that?"

"I can." Margaret smiled. "Hold out your right hand."

Kalia did as instructed. Margaret concentrated on Kalia's palm, tracing a long nailed, weathered finger along invisible lines. They both leaned on the counter for support. Margaret's face remained blank until she finished with a nod.

"You have many journeys ahead of you. Some you will be unable to avoid. You will suffer heartache but become stronger through your experiences. Seek help where you can and accept assistance where offered." She sighed. "You have suffered so much pain already. A girl of your age should never have to witness what you have." Margaret wiped her right eye and continued. "Your... guide? Will assist you through the journeys to come. Its advice will be invaluable." Margaret stopped and massaged her sinuses. "That is all I can tell you."

"It's fine. Thank you for your help." Kalia bowed before grabbing the medallion box and leaving.

\*

Kalia arrived back at the docks, letting out a sigh of relief that the ship hadn't left without her. A bag of raisins, sultanas and dried apricots was looped to the drawstring of her sirwal; she had sold one of the gold statues for the lot and received no change.

Winchester and the Captain were nowhere to be seen.

Kalia climbed up the rope ladder that led to the deck, but before she could set foot on the ship, a drawn cutlass pointed close to her neck. Kalia stopped moving and looked up the blade's length into the single eye of a girl a few years her senior. She had a short crew cut and wore a linen shirt, leather breeches and boots. A bronze plated eye patch with the ships decal carved upon it covered her left eye.

"Kid, I'm not in the mood," she said in irritated Orthodox, a scowl on her face.

Before Kalia could respond, not that she understood the language, Captain Cortain appeared and called over. "Cassidy, what the heck are you playing at? She's our guest."

Cassidy looked back at Cortain, keeping her blade aimed. "You what? Is she freebooting?" her voice was less aggressive around the Captain.

"She's paying for passage to Chivralor. It's worth it." Cortain fixed Cassidy with a gaze. She lowered her weapon and Kalia exhaled.

Captain Cortain gestured her below decks and called towards his cabin. "Winchester! Could you give Miss Kalia the grand tour and show her to her quarters?"

A gruff voice came out from the Captain's cabin, "Yeah sure, comin' Captain." Winchester waddled out and motioned Kalia towards a deck hatch, changing to Suveerian. "This way, Mum."

*"Did he mean to say madam?"* Kalia thought.

Winchester and Kalia walked a short flight of steps below the decks. A few candle lanterns illuminated the oaken surroundings, revealing a curtained-off area at the bow of the deck. A few men and women, dressed in practical sailing fatigues, passed them by. Winchester mentioned that they were part-time crew assistants; employees who kept the ship in shape but rarely, if ever, joined in skirmishes or battles. The mention of battles sent a cold brush against the back of Kalia's neck. She noticed many brass pipes snaking along the ceiling and into the floor.

Footsteps sounded behind the two. A tall man, wearing a bronze chest plate with a beard the length of Kalia's forearm, sauntered towards them. He was hunched over to keep his head from knocking on the ceiling.

Winchester waved to the man. "This big man is Haldor. Tundrashian. Don't let he big size pull you off, he's got a gold heart." Winchester changed to Orthodox. "Haldor, this is Kalia. We're just giving her a ride to Chivralor."

Haldor smiled and nodded. "Good evening Miss Kalia." His speech was deep, heavily accented and slow. Kalia bowed.

Winchester showed Kalia past two sets of bunk beds. On the wall next to one was the funnelled end of one of the brass pipes. Winchester explained that it was a speaking tube.

They continued to the kitchen; a cramped quarter with a small gas stove, a tin sink connected to a water tank and a larder. All three parts were squeezed together around the room, which meant that there was barely enough room for anyone to work. A clean-shaven man in a white vest, leather breeches and a red cloth bandana was peeling a potato. His arms were covered with tattoos; silhouettes of blades and stars. He smiled and raised his knife.

"Ello young lady."

"Tricky, this is Kalia. She'll be travelling with us and I'm playin' tour guide."

"Poor you. We've got potato stew for dinner," said Tricky.

"Sounds delicious. Is there enough for one more?"

Tricky nodded. "There's always enough."

Winchester turned to Kalia. "This is Tricky, our cook and... erm." he paused and waved his hand around, muttering something to Tricky in Orthodox.

Tricky raised both hands, crossed them over each other and the potato along with the peeler in his hands disappeared. He then put his hands behind his back and brought up two potatoes in each hand. "The word you're looking for is illusionist... and I haven't a clue what the Suveerian term is. Try reading those dictionaries of yours."

Winchester rolled his eyes.

Kalia smiled and bowed.

The tour continued down to the cannon quarters. Four semi-auto cannons, two either side, sat with their barrels pointed outside. A padded seat was connected to each one with a lever used to load the cannon from a gravity fed stack. Despite ample opportunity for seawater to enter, the area around the cannons was kept clean. The smell of gunpowder fogged the entire room. The bathroom was located at the stern of this deck.

The bottom deck was the cargo hold, half empty and pitch black. White rope hammocks were set up where there was space. As best he could, Winchester explained, that the hammocks were for the part-time crew. The engine room was located at the stern of this deck, but Kalia didn't get to see much of it.

Winchester concluded the tour by bringing Kalia up to the second deck and pointing to the curtained-off area.

"You will share with Cassidy and Nima."

"Thanks again."

"You safe."

The curtain opened up and a woman with bronze skin, ponytailed hair and purple eyes came out. Her iris and pupils shared the same purple colour. She was Dhalsheran. She wore a pair of black, baggy, ankle-length sirwal, a black vest tunic and a purple scarf that covered up the lower part of her face. A pair of twin dao sabres hung at her waist.

"Ah Nima. I wondered where you'd gone."

"Good evening Winchester. I overheard that this lady is to be our guest?"

"Her name's Kalia, she's paying good, yadda yadda. Is there a spare bunk on your side?"

"Yes, two in fact. She may pick either one."

"Right. Hope your Suveerian's good. I'm gonna check in with the Captain before we set sail."

Winchester saluted, then plodded upstairs.

Nima approached Kalia and examined her up and down. "My name is Nima, I am a medic." Her Suveerian was much better than Winchester's.

She pointed to Kalia's leg and Kalia reluctantly let her take a closer look. Afterwards, Nima shook her head and pointed to a stool next to a cupboard. Kalia sat down and extended her bitten leg. Nima removed the bandages; she didn't so much as wince when she saw how septic the wound had become. Kalia's hand covered her mouth. With all the other aches, pains and adrenaline rushes during her journey, she hadn't noticed the state of her calf muscle.

Nima got up and grabbed a bottle full of clear fluid. Kalia braced herself for what was to come. Nima soaked cotton wool in the spirit and swabbed Kalia's wolf bite. Kalia squinted and sucked air through her teeth; the stinging sensation was worse than the first time the wound had to be disinfected. Three balls of cotton wool were expended in the process.

Once cleaned, Nima applied fresh bandages. The smell of acrid disinfectant overwhelmed the warm scent of gravy, carrots and potatoes drifting in from the kitchen.

Nima made a gesture to Kalia, tipping her hand in front of her mouth. A drink? Kalia nodded. Nima passed through the curtain and out of sight.

Kalia scanned the bunk beds, not knowing which one was hers for the night. Fatigue had drained her. The covers were clean and the plush beds looked comfortable. "*No, no, stay awake. It would be rude to fall asl...*"

*

Nima passed through the curtain with a steaming tin mug of tea. She found Kalia passed out on her bunk and smiled.

Nima pulled up a stool and placed the hot tea in a wooden cup holder, something the Captain had built into his generals' bunks. Before sitting down, Nima fetched a book from a basket. Time passed as Nima read a romance novel set in Orikai, translated to Orthodox, whilst Kalia rested peacefully.

A harsh chime rang out, snapping Kalia awake. She scrambled up and apologised, but Nima put a hand on her shoulder, shook her head, then nodded towards the curtain.

Nima lead Kalia towards the kitchen, where Tricky was serving up stew. He welcomed Kalia and Nima with a smile and handed them a bowl each. Cassidy passed them with her own bowl of hot stew, her face flinty.

"It may look like slop, but it's nutritious and hopefully tastes great," he said.

Nima gave a barely audible chuckle. "Tricky, your food is always delicious. That's why we always have you cook."

"Heh, when you put it like that it makes all the cooking worth it."

Nima blushed underneath her scarf, something she hoped Kalia didn't notice. They collected their food and Nima took Kalia up to the Captain's cabin.

To Nima's knowledge, it was the first time Kalia had seen the inside of the cabin. In the corner to her right was the helm. Thick plate bronze covered the corner where the helm was and a riveted port window was fitted in front of the wheel. It seemed the Captain sailed the ship from a well-guarded room. A round mahogany table surrounded by folding wooden chairs sat in the middle of the cramped chamber. Charts and maps had been carelessly tossed to one side. Behind the table, at the stern, was a bed no different in size than the bunk beds below.

Cassidy was slouched at the table, casually chowing down. Cortain stood at the seat near his bed and gestured to Nima and Kalia to have a seat. Nima glided down next to Cassidy and Kalia followed on next to her. The rest of the crew joined shortly afterwards. Since there weren't enough seats, the Captain allowed Tricky to take his.

Cortain slumped down onto his bed with the bowl of stew Tricky brought up for him. None of the part-time crew were there; they ate the same stew as everyone else, but in the decks below.

Nima kept her scarf on whilst she ate; keeping her mouth covered whilst guiding her spoon through a small gap between the wraps of fabric. As with most of Tricky's dishes, warm, succulent flavour packed with herbs and spices soothed the taste buds with every spoonful.

Nima noticed Kalia's enthusiastic eating, devouring every last drop quickly as if she hadn't eaten for days. "*Not entirely surprising, bless her.*"

When everyone had finished, the Captain rose from his bed and fetched five tin tumblers and a bottle of clear, dark brown liquid. Having filled the tumblers, he handed them to all except Nima and Tricky; hesitating on Kalia.

"Is it a bad idea to start em young on the hard stuff?" Cortain asked.

"Yes," replied everyone in the room.

Cortain shrugged. "If she's curious enough, she can have a sip of mine."

Cortain stood at the table between Tricky and Nima. He raised his tumbler and announced, "Cheers everyone."

*

Smoke billowed out of the twin exhausts on the stern of the ship. Multiple releases of steam and the vibrations from the ship's propellers brought everything to a buzzing tension.

The Procrastination sailed out of the dock at a speed that was almost painful to watch. Kalia stood by the rail during the ship's leave. She kept her gaze on her home country as it moved further and further away. Her face remained straight to hide the nauseating swirl of nervousness in her stomach.

Later that night, Kalia lay on the top bunk, above Nima. A candle gave dim light for Kalia to read her grandfather's journal. Cassidy slept on the top bunk opposite. Nima, still wearing her scarf, read a book of her own below Kalia. The waves, the creak of the ship and its low rumbling steam engine were the only sounds.

Kalia was about to start a chapter but felt queasy from sea sickness within a minute. She closed the journal, blew out the candle and shut her eyes.

Kalia slept, cradling her rucksack and its contents.

*

Fresh salty air mixed with the scent of stale wood awoke Kalia. It was the first time she had slept in a bed so comfortable. Her face was damp with tears from the dream she'd had.

In Kalia's dream, she was in a small, featureless room containing only a bed. Upon the bed were her parents. She didn't barrel into their arms, for fear of ending the dream early, but sat between them and rested her head on Gashaan's shoulder. They embraced her but said nothing. A door of light opened up, slowly consuming the room. Kalia held both her parents close and told them how much she loved them before the light filled the room. Just before she woke up, she caught a glimpse of her parents' faces.

But they were featureless, just like the misshapen in Clibousten.

Kalia wiped her eyes and rolled out of bed. Nima slept peacefully on her bed but Cassidy's covers were crumpled as she lay bunched up, clutching her pillow.

Kalia plodded up the stairs and opened the watertight brass hatch. She shivered; a damp breeze swept her face as she stepped upon the top deck. The sky was cloudy and dull.

Winchester leaned on the side, gazing out at the sea. Kalia joined him. He was drinking coffee from a tin cup and regarded her with a nod and a "Good morning". Kalia returned the greeting.

The following silence lasted half a minute.

"Did you sleep well?" asked Winchester out of the blue. Judging by his grasp of the pronunciation, his Suveerian had improved a little.

"Yes, the beds are very comfortable." she replied.

"Good. We should arrive Chivralor, four days' time. Tricky has plan for our sheets." and his Suveerian returned to a mess.

*"At least he's still trying,"* Kalia thought with a smile. "Anything I can do to help?" she asked.

Winchester made a noise as he sipped from his coffee. He wiped his moustache and cleared his throat. "Maybe later. Now I teach you Orthodox?"

Kalia smiled. "Yes please."

Winchester educated Kalia on many helpful sayings and phrasings until a familiar chime came up from a speaking tube; Breakfast. Everyone ate at the captain's table just like the previous night.

Tricky served a thick oat substance cooked with water called porridge; a tad bland on its own but delicious with the addition of the sultanas and dried apricots Kalia had procured in the port town. According to Winchester, porridge was usually cooked with milk, but since milk was likely to go sour during their long voyage, they would have to make do with water. As least that's what she thought he'd said. Kalia didn't miss Pitacha bread. Her mind swam with the possibilities of better meals once she arrived in Chivralor.

Captain Cortain spoke between mouthfuls. "So we have a guest and yet we haven't even made the proper introductions." He placed a hand on his chest. "Captain Theodore Cortain of The Procrastination."

Kalia smiled and placed a hand on her chest in return whilst Winchester translated.

Cortain steepled his fingers and crossed his legs, resting them on the table. "Winchester, if you would be so kind as to ask Kalia to introduce herself and tell us what brings her out alone to our ship."

All eyes fell on Winchester, who sighed. "Look, I can get her to say her name, but she may not wanna talk that much. Everyone's business is their own, we all know that."

Captain Cortain responded. "I can understand that, I'm just curious to know how a girl of such a young age came across enough funds for a trip out of the country. I'm even more curious as to how she just so happened to turn up when our ship was at port."

Winchester grunted and asked Kalia what had brought her out to the Galhadeen docks on her own. She gazed at the table. Everyone's eyes were on her. She shook her head. Winchester reassured her before turning to the others.

"There's your answer."

Haldor spoke up. "Suveer-Kotol is land of much bloodshed. There is little reason why people leave for peaceful shores."

"If we're getting paid, does it matter? Maybe her turning up was a coincidence," said Cassidy, polishing off the last of her breakfast.

Before anyone else could speculate, Kalia arose from the table with an empty bowl. "Thank you Tricky," she said in surprisingly good Orthodox.

"Err-I... my pleasure," said Tricky, taken aback by Kalia's politeness.

Kalia bowed and took her leave from the Captain's cabin.

Outside, the cloudy sky had parted; differing shades of blue clashed with each other in every direction.

Meanwhile, back in the cabin, Cortain was in mid conversation with the crew.

"I'm just saying it seems a little odd. Maybe I am paranoid, but she has a backpack and I think it's best if we keep an eye on her," he said.

"She is a good girl. Far too damaged and weary to cause problems. I will check her condition to see if she can help out later," said Nima.

"Cheers Nima, I know it sounds rude, but everyone on board a ship's gotta pull their weight." Cortain stood up, cleared his throat and addressed his crew. "Lads and lasses, to your stations."

"Aye-aye Captain," said everyone else in unison.

*

Later that morning, with clear sunny skies, Kalia was sent to the cargo hold to fetch a mop and bucket. Nima had medically cleared her and, according to what Winchester had translated, she could remove the bandages tomorrow. For the rest of the day, she swabbed the decks. The menial labour was nowhere near as bad as the fields. No one yelled at her for slowing down and the sea breeze was cool and refreshing, if a little chilly.

Once the decks were done, Kalia was sent down to the kitchen to help Tricky prepare lunch. Tricky was patient and educational with Kalia, demonstrating a few chopping techniques and pointing to a clock to show how long to cook an item for. Today's lunch was pearl barley with tinned fish and dried kale. The pearl barley took an hour to boil, but the end result was tasty, at least by Kalia's standards. Everyone ate at their own bunks this time.

The rest of the day consisted of chores and language lessons. The Captain called Kalia to his cabin as the sun dipped its backside into the sea. When she arrived, he gave her the wheel. Kalia steered the ship whilst Winchester directed her, his eyes focused on the charts.

The idea of steering such a gigantic vessel excited Kalia at first, but she found it boring after thirty minutes. Cortain took over and Kalia was beckoned down into the kitchen once more; potato stew again.

In the same manner as the previous night, everyone but Cortain fetched a wooden bowl, got a ladleful of stew and sat down at a set table in the Captain's cabin.

Cortain addressed Winchester. "So is our guest ready to tell us bit more about herself?"

Winchester sighed. "Cortain…"

"It is okay," said Kalia, standing up. "I will talk."

Cortain gave a curt nod before asking. "First I would like to know why you're on your own. Where are your parents?"

Kalia glanced at Winchester; he nodded back, ready to fill in the gaps of her language if needed.

She closed her eyes, exhaled and said, "My parents are gone."

Everyone stopped eating. The room fell uncomfortably silent.

"I'm sorry. I didn't mean to bring up something like that. We just wanted to make sure no one had posted a missing person's notice," said Cortain. He paused to give Kalia and Winchester time to translate. "More importantly, your backpack," he thumbed at his back. "What's in it?"

Again Kalia paused. "Survival gear and… my grandfather's journal." Her answer was slow as she struggled to remember her Orthodox under pressure.

Cortain rested his head on his interlaced hands, deep in thought. A moment passed.

"You're half right," he said as he reached for something under the table. He lifted up Kalia's backpack and gently tossed it to her. Kalia grabbed the bag, her mouth half open and her eyes wide. Cortain explained with words and gestures. "I had Cassidy bring this up. The relics I'm not bothered about, but what is in the box?"

Kalia clutched the bag straps tightly.

She exhaled in frustration. Unable to communicate properly, she turned to Winchester. Her speech was quiet but quick and frantic. Winchester gestured to Kalia to slow down. When Winchester had absorbed enough information, he explained.

"Accordin' to Miss Kalia here, the box contains her grandfather's keepsake; a medallion."

Cortain gazed at his empty bowl of stew. "Open it."

Kalia starred at Cortain. "No," she said.

"I have to know if the box holds an explosive or a poison. If you do not show me what's inside, I will throw you overboard." Cortain's voice was stern and his face bore a cold frown.

Once Winchester had finished translating, Kalia scrambled to get the little wooden box from her bag. She placed it on the table and opened it. Everyone leaned in to get a closer look. Kalia pointed to the beautiful medallion that lay inside, yelling in her native tongue.

Cortain's hand covered his face in shame. She packed away her box and stormed out of the cabin.

"She says…" Winchester started.

"Yes, Winchester I know…" Cortain finished.

*

Kalia threw herself up on the top bunk bed. She interlaced her fingers behind her head and huffed. *"I've just told them something that could cost me my life."* She turned on her side and held her rucksack close. *"So what happens now?"*

*

"Nima, can you go talk her?" asked Cortain.

"I can try. Once I've finished my dinner," Nima said.

"Did you have to bring it up here? Why didn't you ask her earlier?" asked Winchester.

Cortain stood up and paced the room. "For a while, I didn't think it mattered. You all know how bloody awful Suveer-Kotol is, why not help someone escape?" Cortain turned his attention to his crew. "But then I felt paranoid. It just seemed odd, how a girl came across jewellery and items worth so much money and yet she didn't have her parents to see her off? I have you lot to look out for. If she was a threat, I had to know." Cortain walked over to a desk at the head of his bed. He opened a drawer and lifted out the silver necklace with the sapphire gem. "I guess this had a lot to do with me hesitating… Nima, can you ask Kalia to meet me on deck when… erm… you know, she doesn't want to kill me for…"

"Yes Captain," said Nima, as she polished off the last mouthful of stew.

*

Kalia heard the deck hatch open and footsteps coming down the stairs. She remained on her bed, facing the wall.

"Kalia?" came a soft accented voice.

"Hello Nima," said Kalia with little enthusiasm.

Nima said nothing. After a minute of silence, Kalia turned over to see Nima standing next to her bunk. She didn't look angry or sad, but offered her hand to Kalia, who took it as an invitation of apology.

Kalia shifted off her bunk and Nima gestured her to follow.

Kalia was led to the top deck where Cortain stood at the bow, gazing out at the ocean. It was night time with a clear sky, bright stars and the blue moon of the awakening season in broad view.

Kalia approached the Captain, who turned around and beckoned for her to join him. Nima took her leave and Kalia stood beside the Captain, who pointed at something in the distance. He handed Kalia his spyglass. She looked through it, only for Cortain to take it away, extend it, then give it back again. This time, when Kalia gazed through it, she could see miles ahead. At first she was confused by what she was supposed to be looking at; nothing but darkness loomed ahead. But then Kalia saw it. A giant eel with ten glowing pearl eyes and sapphire skin, gazing up at the moon. It sang a single long note that rose in pitch before dropping in tone and fading out.

The eel sank below the water and seconds later leapt out of the sea, before plunging back down with a crash, sending out miniature tidal waves that wobbled the ship.

A brighter smile rose on Kalia's face.

*

Another early morning welcomed Kalia back from her sleep. Three more days of sailing left. She wasn't going to miss the ebb and flow of the waves; it made her queasy, unbalanced below decks and she found it impossible to read her journal.

Kalia ascended for some fresh air and once again found Winchester standing on the far port side, gazing out at the sea, coffee in hand. The sea air was much colder now. Kalia shuddered and rubbed her arms from a stray breeze. A low fog covered the horizon. She stood beside Winchester and he nodded in greeting.

"Good morning," he said in Orthodox.

Kalia responded in kind.

Winchester switched back to Suveerian. "I want to apologise if we caused you any harm last night."

"Apology accepted," Kalia said with a nod.

"So today I…" he changed back to Orthodox suddenly. "What in…?" Winchester squinted at something in the distance. He withdrew a spyglass attached to his belt and eyed a ship coming towards them. "Ah never mind, it's another pirate ship. They won't bother us."

Kalia's attention turned towards the approaching ship. It looked to be as big as The Procrastination.

It turned to face them, port side on.

A dull *thomp* and a small puff of fire and smoke came from the ship.

Something round hurtled through the air towards them.

A second later, it exploded in the water near the bow of the ship, rocking it from side to side.

Winchester cursed under his breath. "God dammit!" He yelled into every speaking tube on deck. "Battle stations, we're under attack!"

*

Kalia was sent to the Captain's cabin, where the bronze plated panelling near the helm wheel would provide the best protection.

Everyone moved quickly but efficiently; Cortain steered the ship, Cassidy and Haldor manned the cannons, Tricky and Nima stayed up top keeping an eye and hand on the sails, Winchester stood above the cabin manning a massive harpoon turret.

All Kalia could hear was the frequent boom of the cannons. The ship rocked in a nauseating fashion. The impact of stone cannonballs smashing into the hull made Kalia scream and cower.

Cortain called over. "Hide under the table if you have to. Just hold onto... and I just realised you can't understand most of what I'm saying..." his voice trailed off.

"I go under table. Yes?" answered Kalia in her fractured Orthodox, crawling underneath the table.

Cortain tilted his head in agreement. He yelled into one of the speaking tubes. "Winchester! Status report."

Winchester's voice echoed back. "They're about to pass us, turn full rudder to port... now!"

Cortain gritted his teeth and put all of his force into turning the helm wheel. Kalia watched with frightened eyes, holding tightly to the table leg. For a moment everything went quiet.

The air splitting booms started again.

"Got one of the bastard's cannons, Captain!" shouted Cassidy from the pipe.

"Nice one, keep it up!" Cortain responded.

A sudden collision shook Kalia's world. Her ears rang. When she regained her bearing, she glanced up. Shattered glass littered the floor. There was a small dent in the wall. Cortain was face down on the floor, still moving but groggy. Kalia scurried over to him. She rolled him over and supported his head. His eyes were wide in delirium.

"Dang it. Captain, you okay down there?" cried Winchester from above.

Kalia ran over to the tube. "The Captain is down. He is dizzy."

"Kalia! Erm… quick, grab wheel."

Kalia jumped to the helm and stopped it from turning. "Got it."

"Good, now turn it your left and going."

Kalia exerted her strength into turning the wheel.

"Stop! Now turn it back until you straight… that is it."

Winchester instructed Kalia during the battle, struggling with his Suveerian under stress. Under his orders, Kalia called down the first tube on the left for Nima. She didn't hear a response.

The blasts were much louder now. Kalia's heart thundered in her chest. She stood to the right of the wheel whilst steering.

Kalia received frequent updates from Winchester, Cassidy and Haldor. She had a hard time understanding the latter two.

The cabin door suddenly flew open and Nima burst in. She knelt by the Captain and put a vial of something under his nose. He hacked, coughed and got to his feet.

"Thank you, I will take it from here," Cortain said with a smile.

Kalia nodded and moved aside. Cortain contacted Winchester. "I'm back. How are things up there?"

Winchester's voice bellowed from the tube, "Got the sum bitch, harpoon cannon in the ass cheek. Reel 'em in Captain."

"They better bloody well surrender." Cortain wound up a big cog and pulled a breaker. A sliding metal clank followed by a rhythmic ticking sounded out. A structure of gears and pulleys built into the central section of the wall and leading up to the cabin roof started moving. Cortain opened all the tubes and addressed his crew. "Everyone prepare yourselves. We are about to do some boarding."

A celebratory cheer echoed into the cabin.

*

Cortain and Nima drew their swords and charged outside. Kalia looked on from the cabin doorway. Cortain, Nima, Haldor and Cassidy had taken cover by the port side deck rail cover.

The other ship drew closer, gradually pulled in by the harpoon's winch. Cortain armed himself with a gun that had a stubby handle and two bronze barrels.

"Winchester, are they surrendering?" he asked.

Winchester dropped down from the roof of the cabin. "I didn't see no white flag."

"Bugger." Cortain rallied the rest of his crew. "Get ready, looks like we're in for a scrap. Kalia. Wheel. Full left!"

Kalia grabbed the helm and turned it anticlockwise with all her force. A gunshot rang out and *pinged* off something metallic above. The bronze chain connecting the two ships trembled but held fast. The way Cortain's ship was turning meant that the stern of the enemy vessel would face the port side of Cortain's ship.

"Hey Winchester, do you think maybe next time you could hit the other ship somewhere away from its arse-end?" asked the Captain.

"You try firin' a one-shot cannon whilst the other side is trying to gun you down."

"Point taken. Get ready everyone, here they come."

Kalia's grip on the wheel tightened as the enemy's stern approached. The captain's cabin cast a shadow over Cortain's deck.

Winchester called to Kalia to flip the breaker to stop the winch. For a moment, Kalia stared, dumbfounded, at the mess of levers and switches. On a guess she pulled one, vaguely remembering which one Cortain had pulled earlier. The cogs and gears stopped turning.

Kalia's attention return to the deck outside as a copper ball with a lit fuse flew off the end of the enemy ship and clattered in front of the crew. Haldor leapt towards the grenade, grabbed it and lobbed it back to where it had come from. His speed made Kalia's eyes widen. The bomb exploded in mid-air, above the stern of the enemy ship. Screams from an enemy pirate continued after the deafening blast.

Many rowdy voices howled in berserk rage as five rag-tag pirates jumped on to Cortain's ship. Three women, two men.

The chaos of the melee was insane to keep track of. Kalia's notice was first drawn to Nima. Her twin dao sabres twirled as a thug lunged towards her. He was wearing a bandana, no shirt and patchwork breeches.

Nima blocked his cutlass with one blade then twirled around to cut a swath along his chest with the other. Her technique was like a fast-paced belly dance.

The boom of Cortain's shotgun made Kalia jump, cower and cover her ears. A round of burning buckshot took care of a larger pirate wielding a broadsword, his tanned leather armour couldn't save him.

More bangs as Winchester's revolver blasted a young female pirate's kneecap before she could draw her sword. She collapsed to the ground, clutching her knee whilst she screamed.

By this point, Kalia had curled up in the corner; her hands held tightly over her ears and her eyes squeezed shut.

No more explosions followed, only a few grunts, screams and clashing of bronze. She opened her eyes when she heard Cortain's voice.

"Cassidy! Calm your arse down!" Cortain yelled in controlled irritation. "To those alive but injured, stay down if you want to live."

Kalia crawled out from the gap between the helm wheel and the wall with the big porthole window. She flinched and looked away with a grimace at what she glimpsed. Cassidy was standing over the body of a female pirate she had just butchered; blood soaked the body and deck. Another woman held her gory stump of an arm and screamed.

Cortain straightened up, cupped his hands and shouted. "To the Captain of this vessel: surrender and you will not be harmed."

"He's already dead, Captain," came a familiar voice. Kalia continued to listen.

"Tricky? Is that you?"

"Aye-aye, Captain. The boson's surrendered. The ship's ours."

The Captain sighed. "Nima, could you kindly tend to the injured? Keep your swords at the ready of course."

Nima nodded. "Aye-aye Captain."

*

The part-time pirates, or scubbies, were put to work. A haul of coal, repair plunder, food and a measly amount of gold were brought aboard The Procrastination.

Kalia assisted where she could, but wasn't allowed aboard the other ship. Not that she minded; her legs shook internally from her front row experience of the battle.

The defeated captives were lined up on the deck. Cortain paced back and forth as he preached to them. Kalia had returned topside as he spoke.

"So… does anyone want to tell me why you fired upon our ship? A fellow pirate vessel no less?"

The girl with the blown kneecap spoke up; her hair draped in a tangled mess over a sweat-laced face. "We were after the bounty on one of your crew members."

Cortain looked around at each member of his crew, including Kalia, who he paused on. "Who exactly?"

She pointed. "That Tundrashian, Haldor. He's worth one thousand crests."

Haldor laughed. "That is pathetic money to catch me."

Cortain continued. "What kind of self-respecting pirate attacks one of their kind?"

"We needed the money!" whined the boson; a short, bald man with a pair of pince-nez on the end of his nose.

Tricky spoke up. "He's not lying, Captain- they've barely got enough to repair our damages."

Cortain sighed and massaged the bridge of his nose. "Right then." He paced around in thought for a minute before raising his voice. No one seemed to mind that Kalia had stopped helping to listen.

"Crewmates of The Boddinghide, as it stands you have two options. Either work alongside us as crew for The Procrastination or... I dunno, we'll shoot you."

The girl with the missing hand answered with fury in her tone. "Do you honestly think we'd want to join your crew after that... monster slaughtered our friend? How about you leave us on The Boddinghide to die?"

Cortain stopped pacing and faced the girl, aware of Cassidy's glare, though it might have been a grin. "I'm sorry for any casualties we may have caused, but your Captain fired first and then hid in his cabin. We can leave you aboard The Boddinghide if that's what you want."

Every captive crew member nodded.

"Very well. Tricky, Haldor, can you give them back a little bit of their food and coal. Winchester, would you be so kind as to find the nearest piece of land from here and give them the details?" He cupped his hands and shouted. "Everyone pack up and be ready to leave, we're hauling away."

Kalia resumed helping, hauling a little box to the decks below as a few calls of "Aye-aye Captain" could be heard from all around.

Tricky sung quietly "Oh, me first mate's an arsehole..."

The remaining crew members of The Boddinghide boarded their ship. Winchester left them with directions to an island far off the coast of Suveer-Kotol, which would give them a place to repair their ship and keep warm.

As Kalia finished carrying cargo, she spotted Cortain standing atop his cabin's roof. He kept his eyes on The Boddinghide as it sailed off into the distance.

*

Tricky made a good, hearty brunch with the recently plundered food. Kalia ate her meal slowly. She struggled to keep her hand steady, unable to block out the memories of that day's massacre; Cortain blasting a grown man with his shotgun and the end result of Cassidy cleaving a woman to death. At least when Balshadee killed the masked assassin, it had been quick. More so than ever, death played on her mind.

Kalia's meal of jerky stew looked grotesque all of a sudden; the gravy turning crimson to her eyes.

She returned her bowl to the kitchen and fetched a mop and bucket again- anything to take her mind off today's events.

The notion seemed all too familiar to her.

*

The distraction of yesterday's pirate battle had taken the arrival time back a few hours, but in two days' time, around noon, they would arrive at Sailors' Respite.

Kalia ascended to the top deck to find Winchester sipping his coffee again. She bade him good morning and he nodded back.

"You didn't eat many yesterday," he said in Suveerian. His grasp of the language had improved by leaps and bounds in just a few days. Sort of. "You need strength and we can't throw food here."

"I have seen too much death. But the bloodshed is what disturbs me," Kalia said.

"Yes, Cassidy is a troubled girl, but she is loyal."

"What made you become pirates?"

Winchester paused to sip from his coffee. "Hmm, many of us would rather not say, especially Cassidy. Haldor was a slave. I became a pirate because I was bored."

Kalia raised both eyebrows. "Because you were bored?"

"Yes, I worked my whole life as a navigator for merchant boats. First day of retirement I threw down my, err..." he frowned and mumbled in Orthodox. "What's that word for newspaper?" he resumed in Suveerian. "New fabric and I announced that I was bored. I had no wife to stop me and in three months I was aboard The Procrastination."

"Any regrets?"

Winchester smiled. "None. So, ready to practise more Orthodox?"

Kalia nodded and Winchester educated. He taught her more greetings, compliments and what to order in a restaurant. In particular, she asked him to teach her how to make a specific request.

"You would say 'I. Need. You. To Keep. This. Safe.' Now repeat."

"I need you. To keep. This safe." Kalia responded.

"Not bad. You will be speaking all the languages in the world soon."

A chime blared out of the speaking tubes; Tricky calling for breakfast again.

*

The last two sailing days passed without incident.

On Kalia's final night aboard the ship, the crew threw her a leaving celebration. Despite the Captain's best efforts, she refused to touch a drop of rum.

The next morning, Kalia was assisting with the rigging when a cry came from Cortain's cabin.

"Land ho!"

Kalia turned around to see what the Captain was yelling about. In the far distance was a patch of dull, dark green, upon which sat the stonework of villages, exuding plumes of smoke.

They had finally reached Chivralor.

Tricky popped up from the kitchen and ascended to the crow's nest. He moved with grace, executing jumps and bounds with acrobatic finesse. He was inside the tub at the top within fifteen seconds. Kalia couldn't make out what he was doing up there. Tricky threw a white sheet that expanded to cover the entire black signature flag. The sheet stayed in place and Tricky remained in the crow's nest, squinting in concentration and muttering something under his breath.

The Procrastination passed ships flying the Chivralor flag; navy vessels. None fired or attempted to flag down Cortain's ship. Kalia was granted an extended break to view the ship pulling into dock from the top deck. What she saw made her jaw hang. In the sky, she saw flying ships; not just one, but eight. Some were elevated by gigantic balloons of canvas whilst others were lifted by many, many sets of grand brass propellers, spinning at blurring speeds. Her grandfather had shown her one from a book in her younger days. To see this many at once almost made Kalia lose balance.

Cortain's ship pulled into an old, filthy, run-down port on a small island called Sailors' Respite. The port, whilst not completely lawless, was a popular hang-out for pirates and smugglers alike.

It dawned on Kalia that she would have to say goodbye. She returned to her bunk bed to pack up her belongings.

When she reached the top deck, Cortain's crew were waiting for her, all lined up and smiling. Even Cassidy managed a smirk.

Winchester stepped forward. "Miss Kalia. On behalf of Cortain's crew, we would like to say thank you. You pulled your weight and helped us when we needed it."

Kalia was beaming as she fought back tears; Winchester's Suveerian was at its very best.

"We can take you no further. We are wanted in Chivralor for piracy. Cortain has agreed to escort you to a ferry headed for Valordom, the capital city. For now, this is goodbye. But if you ever need our services, drop a letter at a tavern called the Smoky Wind."

Winchester turned to his crewmates and hollered. "Send her off. Half a cheer for Kalia."

Everyone but Kalia said. "Hip-hip hoo!"

As Cortain led Kalia off the ship, Cassidy asked, "So what did Winchester say to the girl?"

Tricky answered. "He said Cassidy talks with her fanny."

"I will end you!" she yelled.

*

The streets of the boondocks, known as Gimler's port, were muddy and depressing. Beggars in tatty rags of wool and tartan snored in the streets. The buildings were either derelict or filthy with damp, built from interlacing blocks of clay, called bricks, with tiled roofs and wood-framed windows. Some of the better off buildings had brass framing and gothic style murals. Shady characters eyeballed Cortain and Kalia as they walked by. One such character bumped into Cortain and apologised. Cortain responded by drawing his cutlass.

"Give it back," he ordered.

The vagrant looked flustered. "Ay? Oim sarry mate but I ain't-"

"Now." Cortain's voice was cold.

The pickpocket handed over a few silver coins called crests. Cortain kept his sword raised.

"And the other thing."

The pickpocket groaned and handed over the silver necklace embedded with a sapphire. Kalia was surprised Cortain still had it on him. Cortain concluded the encounter by swiftly punching the vagrant in the face. The vagrant landed on his backside with a wet slap, clutching his nose.

Kalia and Cortain tromped through more streets until they reached the only shop that didn't look like someone had painted it with filth. A polished navy blue background with shiny gold letters read:

*Quintoneers Jewellers.*

Cortain raised a finger and asked Kalia to "Wait here," before going inside. Kalia's Orthodox was good enough that she understood. She leaned against the brickwork wall of the shop and rubbed her arms to keep warm.

Ten minutes later, Cortain departed the shop, the edge of a burlap bag bulging from beneath his jacket. He smiled at Kalia and they continued their journey.

They arrived at a motorized taxi rank on the outskirts of the port town. A combustion engine sat on the back of a roofed carriage with large rubber and timber wheels. The driver was squashed into his seat at the front, judging by how he was hunched up.

Cortain hailed the driver. "How much to get this lady to the Petredi port town ferry?"

"Ten silver crests," said the driver.

Cortain handed over a bank note from within the burlap bag and got a few gold crests in return.

Kalia got into the carriage; the interior was dark but held shimmering purple velvet cushioning and little red curtains at the windows. Cortain didn't follow- instead he pushed a few bank notes into Kalia's hand.

"You not come?" she asked with worry.

Cortain shook his head. "You take care now."

Before Kalia could protest, a pop and bang came from the engine and the driver pulled away.

Kalia kept her eyes on Cortain, who saluted as the motor carriage drove her away.

*

## One month later, city of Valordom.

Kalia pressed a brass button beside the door. A shrill bell sounded from inside.

Kalia had found a place to stay at an orphanage. The nun who oversaw everything there, a Sister Bannybush, reluctantly agreed to take care of her after Kalia bribed away most of the money she made from her treasure.

Kalia hadn't realised how strict Sister Bannybush was on independent errands, but she had successfully escaped from the orphanage grounds to be here. She had disposed of her filthy Suveerian clothing shortly after joining the orphanage and was now wearing an ankle-length skirt, white blouse and a new pair of shoes. Over the past month, she had improved her grasp of the Orthodox language. By chance, she became acquainted with the local homeless. It was a vagrant gentleman by the name of Gary who directed Kalia to this house, or first floor maisonette, to use the proper term.

Footsteps thumped down the stairs from inside. A metal click later and the door opened. Standing in the porch was a short man in his late twenties with black, buzz cut hair, wearing a white, buttoned shirt, smart trousers and with a pair of brass goggles affixed to his forehead.

"Erm, can I help?" asked the man.

"Are you Charlie Blunt?" asked Kalia.

"Yes, is everything alright?" Charlie looked sceptical, his eyes darted left and right along the street. "Is this an ambush?"

Kalia lifted a wooden box and pushed it into Charlie's hand. "Can you keep this safe? From everyone and anyone?"

"Hang on, how do I know this isn't a…"

"Please," Kalia added.

Charlie took the box and scrutinised it. He went to open it, but Kalia put a hand on its lid. "Can you keep it safe?" Kalia's eyes were pleading.

Charlie met Kalia's gaze. "Yes I can."

"Promise?"

"I can keep it hidden. I can promise that."

"Thank you."

Kalia bowed and disappeared down the street before Charlie could say any more.

Charlie closed the door to his home and jogged upstairs. When he stepped inside his lounge, newly furnished, he put his ear up to the box. Silence. He gave the container a little shake. Something clinked inside. Charlie opened the box.

He gazed, mesmerised at what was inside, before closing the box again.

Charlie sauntered over to his bookshelf and pulled on a false book. Something went click. Charlie knelt down and removed the large loosened kickboard, placing the box in the dark hideaway beneath the bookshelf.

# Epilogue
## Grand Viziah's palace, Jolduru, Suveer-Kotol.

Every day, he spent an hour looking out at the city from his chamber. The palace was built from white marble and furnished with silk and gold, the ceilings were high and the window he gazed from was bigger than most two storey houses. He wore a pair of circular glasses with lenses so black no one could see his eyes. His head was bald and featured his birth emblem; a four-pointed star of curved yet sharp lines, the centre of which looked like an all-seeing eye. Thick, dark grey stubble coated his chin. His cassock was a brilliant white, trimmed with gold. A gold metal crest embedded with jewels of varying colours was attached to the back of the robe.

A knock came from the gigantic doors.

"Enter," he said.

A man in military uniform entered. "Master Jebedias Mahgzeer. We have found Fenshal Rubi."

"He's alive? Impressive… bring him in."

Two guards wearing mouth masks brought in a beaten, filthy man in a torn, blood-soaked cassock. They shoved him to his knees. The man bowed his head, unable to look Jebedias in the eye.

Jebedias waved to the guards whilst keeping his gaze on Fenshal. "Leave us, please," he asked.

The guards left the room.

"So how long did you continue to run after you failed your mission?" asked Jebedias calmly.

"M-master…" Fenshal's voice was weak.

"Do you know the meaning of the word 'discreet'?"

"I… you told me to kill if I must."

"Ah, so you remembered that, but you forgot what 'discreet' means. I gave you this mission because you have a way with words and people. You are manipulative and I thought you perfect for the task. Instead, not only did you kill a girl's parents, a mountain dweller and a slum's innkeeper, but you also lost your entire team to your own incompetence."

Fenshal's jaw dropped. For a second, he mouthed words of disbelief that never formed sounds. Finally, he managed a sentence. "I-it was the Misshapen; they attacked us in a town that rests in a crater. F-forgive me Master…"

Jebedias slowly paced towards a sword rack on the wall. "You are forgiven."

He picked two backswords off the rack and tossed one down at Fenshal's knees. Fenshal glanced at the blade and looked up in confusion.

Jebedias gave his sword a few swings before he gestured to the other sword. "Well… pick up the blade. If you can best me in a sword fight, you can take my place."

Fenshal grabbed the blade. He tried and failed to keep a brave face as he spoke. "I-I have but one question. What happened to that town in the crater? W-why are its people in… that condition?"

"That's two questions. But this… town you speak of was Clibousten. It was not a town but a village. It was a site where

118

fifteen years ago we conducted an experiment on Astral magic. We wanted to open a portal to another dimension. The contorted shape of the village, the inhabitants and the crater it now rests in are all a result of the experiment."

"But that was in the Galhadeen region. How did you manage to conduct such a thing under the eyes of their government? Why isn't the village on any map we have today?"

Jebedias smiled and raised his blade. "Defeat me and I may just tell you. That is, if you don't kill me first. Quoshtaligh!"

With Quoshtaligh meaning 'Have at you!' Jebedias lunged forward. Fenshal parried the blow but was forced back by quick, graceful strikes. Jebedias remained stony-faced as he fought, showing no excitement, though Fenshal swore he spotted a hint of boredom. Jebedias made every stab and swipe seem effortless. For the first few seconds of the battle, their flexentite swords clashed, till Jebedias spoke mid-fight.

"I sent our troops, spies and experts in astral magic to Galhadeen through gaps in the enemy's defence and via the sea. Galhadeen's military has some of the worst leadership and tactical prowess I've ever seen. Pay attention!"

Jebedias noticed Fenshal's distraction, knocked away his upright blade and sliced a gash across Fenshal's arm.

Fenshal's face tightened and his attack grew more aggressive, but reckless. Every time he thought he'd found an opening, his counterattack was thwarted and parried.

"I've foreseen the outcome of every military operation I have put to task, and yet despite knowing the outcome at Clibousten in advance, I still pressed on. I guess I wanted my visions to be wrong. Your defence is pathetic!"

This time, Jebedias sent his blade across Fenshal's cheek, then knelt low and sliced his kneecap, before returning to a defensive vertical base. The move was too quick for Fenshal to keep track of. Splatters of blood soaked the floor around him. Fenshal attempted a desperate lunge but slipped on his own blood. Jebedias sprung back and Fenshal landed awkwardly in a split legged position.

He grimaced, squeezing his eyes shut to hold back tears, but failed to hide the sounds of his sobbing. His sword clattered to the floor. He opened his eyes and looked at Jebedias.

"W-wait, you, you can end this war! You can stop this bloodshed. Why do you let it continue?"

Jebedias' lunge was swift and well-balanced. Fenshal felt a sort of welcome relief when the blade finally pierced his heart.

Jebedias whispered in Fenshal's ear as the life left his body, "Because this world is full of fools and idiots, unfit to breathe, let alone rule."

Fenshal's body slumped to the side.

Jebedias washed his blade in a basin near the sword rack. He replaced the sword, walked up to his desk and pulled a fabric chord fitted underneath the top that ran beneath the floor. A bell rang from outside. Two guards entered. They didn't flinch when they saw the mess on the floor.

"Take his body to the farms. Ensure his remains make good fertiliser. Also send for a cleaner, but ask him to knock before entering."

The guards bowed, lifted Fenshal's body and shuffled out.

A gentle knock came from behind a wall to the left of the giant window. Jebedias stood near to it and stamped his foot three times.

The wall opened up silently. From out of the secret entrance stepped a woman in a white hooded robe with a gold face guard shaped like bare branches, jagged like interlacing cracks of lightning. She removed both items to reveal her long, glimmering blonde hair. Her eyes had golden irises, but her sclera looked like a cloudless sky. She wore a white and brass buckled leather chest plate and a knee-length white skirt, and was equipped with a short sword. The scabbard of the sword was gold with platinum plating, inscribed with a language only herself and Jebedias could read.

"How is progress?" she said in a tongue never heard of; a soft and gentle language that eased the minds of those who heard it.

"No issues. A case of incompetence has set us back a small way. But I have foreseen the dimensional key's destination."

"Shall I make plans to leave?"

"Not yet. In my vision I saw… something else."

"Go on."

"In the country of Chivralor, I saw not only the new location of the dimensional key but also a scythe for crossing the dimensions."

"Then I should make haste?"

"That is entirely up to you. The key won't be going anywhere. The other item however has not… arrived yet."

"Then I shall leave anyway. No offence, but this country disgusts me."

"None taken, you know the feeling is mutual. The scythe is of Infernium sorcery and…" his face remained blank as he paused to remember, "you will need to seek the help of a gadgeteer detective." Jebedias sniffed, grunted and leaned on his desk, his face still unflinching.

"Are you ok? Is it the precognition?"

"I am fine. Are you well informed of the task at hand?"

"Yes. As long as there is a ship ready to take me. You know how much the people of Jolduru dislike women travelling alone."

Jebedias cleared his throat. "I will send word and a travel partner. Your boat will leave from the north docks. Please excuse me, I must meditate."

"Farewell. May Altumeria guide your will."

## **War and Conviction**
## **Year 112, Era of Invention**

*It started with the murder of a queen*

*It continued on the flames of conflicting beliefs*

*It will end when they finally let go of both.*

Jakenteem; Suveerian philosopher. Year 10, Era of Invention.

Half a mile wide and constantly bombarded with gun or mortar fire, the No Man's Land of Suveer-Kotol was a hell for anyone sent to fight upon it. Its necron black sludge cut what was once a thriving single city into two warring sides, like a scar that never healed; Jolduru to the west and Galhadeen in the east. Makeshift towers and barricades of timber and scrap metal sheltered cowering figures clutching their rifles and dynamite sticks like a second lifeline; if they weren't covered in mud they were coated in blood.

On either side of No Man's Land was another mile of abandoned homes and businesses, known as the evacuation zone. Almost every building was constructed from duststone; a brown, clay-like material that looks like packed mud. Those built by the wealthier were crafted from limestone or concrete. Camps and bases of operations were set up in this area, preparing and briefing the next troops to send into the carnage.

In an elongated house that used to be a hostel, a group of five soldiers were preparing for their first mission as a unit. They were dressed in light brown uniforms with their trousers tucked into black boots that rose up to just below their knees. Their heads were adorned with armour-plated fezzes.

Four more figures stood statuesque, expressionless and attired in rough-spun, filthy clothing. They did not breathe or blink. They were to be the soldier's meat shields.

Essayn was the commander of the group. A tall male with long, tied-up black hair. His birth emblem was a pair of shields on both cheeks made up of curved, pointed black lines and circles. He surveyed his comrades, spotting stern expressions and fidgety postures. For the sake of morale, he approached each soldier for a pep talk.

He noticed the confidence in Irralla, the only woman of the group. Her black hair was tied up in a loop tail and her birth emblem ran along her jawline. Her focus was on her single-shot, bolt action rifle; cleaning and getting a feel for its weight with little lifting exercises.

"Nervous of the coming battle?" Essayn asked in his deep, gentle voice.

"Do you ask that because I'm a woman?" Irralla asked without looking up.

Essayn blinked with a riveted eyebrow. "I ask all soldiers this. War brings out the fear in man and woman alike."

She smiled. "On the contrary, I look forward to seeing the looks on the Joldies faces as they're killed by a woman."

"Now that's a face I'd love to see," came the laid-back voice of Gudemsha

Gudemsha was a man of thick build in both the shoulder and gut. Sharp black lines wrapped around his neck with an opaque circle on his Adam's apple; his birth emblem. No hair adorned his head. He was slouched against a wall; a scuffed lever action shotgun on his lap.

Essayn nodded. "Good humour boosts morale; keep it up, soldier."

"Blowing up a cluster of Joldies helps too," Gudemsha said, shaking a single stick of dynamite in his hand.

"Ah, yes, you worked the mortars further north, correct?"

"That I did. No Joldie could build a defence I couldn't destroy."

"I'll leave the dynamite with you, then."

Gudemsha saluted, using the dynamite for a hand, and gazed off into space.

Essayn turned to Urshan, who was standing and staring at the reanimations. He appeared to be in his early twenties. His face was unsmiling and taut, he was gripping a gold locket upon a necklace around his neck. His birth emblem was across the back of his neck, shaped like a star, and his black hair was trimmed to a crew cut.

Essayn placed a hand on Urshan's shoulder, giving it a firm squeeze and a little shake. Urshan's gaze looked towards the commander, calmly.

"They won't fall apart or run away. You should take a seat," said Essayn.

"I've met him before," Urshan nodded towards one of the reanimations; an unassuming male of roughly the same age as himself. "He was my comrade."

Essayn removed his hand. "What was his name?"

"Hakmil."

"Hakmil served us in life. We keep his memory and service in death."

Urshan said nothing, just gave an ill-confident nod.

Finally, Essayn approached Kobino, shortest of the group and tenser than a fixed piano wire. He slowly rocked back and forth, an old-fashioned, percussion cap rifle tipped with a bayonet cradled in his arms. The cap rifles were reserved for initiates and weren't as versatile as bolt or lever action rifles. Kobino had only been with the army for two weeks but had fought alongside Irralla and Urshan during a few days on the front line. All three had been lucky to survive every battle up until this point.

Essayn opened his mouth to speak, but a message girl burst through the door to the base. She wore dull brown robes and a head scarf to help blend in with the common duststone buildings during her travels; much like the uniforms of the military.

"Message for Essayn," she said with a salute.

"Speaking."

The girl pulled out a card tube and withdrew a scroll from inside. She read off the message: "Ready your troops and proceed to briefed coordinates in No Man's Land."

"Received. On your way."

The girl saluted once more and disappeared back through the door.

*

No Man's Land was disturbingly quiet, broken only by brief bursts of artillery here and there. Even the most bloodthirsty of combatants needed sleep and saw little point in wasting ammunition firing in the dark, unless someone was stupid enough to try and sneak by the enemy's defensive line.

Everyone relied on their night-adjusted eyes to find shelter in a trench behind a barricade of thick but rotting wood. On the other side was a part of the battlefield referred to in the briefing as the 'chink in the armour'; a slightly less guarded area in the front line, out of mortar fire range.

Their task was to wait for a signal before storming across the field for eight hundred yards. The reanimations would serve as bullet shields. The team's goal was to make it into the enemy's evacuation zone, secure territory and wait for back up. At the time, no one thought to question the lack of forward-thinking. But as they crouched in the bleak darkness of the night time trench; a feeling of doubt spread like burning parchment.

A two-syllabled whistle split the silence. Without a word, the team of five climbed out of the bunker, flanked by the reanimated bodies.

The trek through the many, many yards of thick mud at a brisk pace had the entire team, save for the undead, gasping for breath before they reached the enemy's bunkers. Moving with any form of stealth or grace was impossible as the muck tried to swallow their boots. Kobino tripped over something but quickly regained his footing and marched onwards. The night made traversing worse; though their eyes had adjusted, they still found distant obstacles difficult to navigate. As a result, they had many near collisions with chunks of splintered wood, dipped craters left by mortar impacts and the remains of soldiers felled by bullets and explosives alike. The reanimations had boundless stamina but no concept of pain or obstacles; consequently they ploughed on and into large splints of wood that jammed into their legs and guts.

As the unit approached the small hill leading to the Jolduru evacuation zone, they dropped into a trench and waited. Everyone with a pulse winced and sucked in air as their muscles convulsed involuntarily like the spasmed death throes of an insect. They glanced around in the gloom. Gudemsha could be heard saying "Think we made it?" Something ruptured in the ground above them, sending dirt into the trench. Gunfire erupted from the peak of the hill. Returning gunfire from the team's allies on the far side embedded itself in the timber of the Jolduru soldiers' cover.

There was a break in the action.

"Move! Up and over!" came Essayn's voice at a controlled volume, hoping the enemy wouldn't hear.

The team clambered out of the trench; clawing, boots scraping at the dirt. The reanimations took the lead. Before they could reach the slope, gunfire broke out once more. The reanimations twitched as every direct hit from Jolduru rifle bullets slammed into them, but when they were close enough, they split from the group and directed the opposition's attack and attention onto themselves.

The distraction worked according to plan and after a brief 'last push' climb, the squadron finally broke free from the mud-filled fields and onto solid ground, trailing filth past the architecture of Jolduru, which had more flourishes in its windows and roof corners and richer building materials.

"Heh... ha! Those idiots couldn't hit a sitting bull at ten yards," Gudemsha commented under heavily laboured breath.

"That's because most of our former friends soaked up the gunfire," said Urshan humourlessly.

"W-Well... y-yeah, but they missed us..." Gudemsha's voice wavered.

"We know what you mean, Gudemsha. Let's hope we're the next ones shooting at that bull," said Irralla through gritted teeth.

"Alright, alright- you want to kill a Joldie? Keep moving and you might get the opportunity later," said Essayn

Behind the dull rhythm of marching boots, the battle faded behind them. Urshan muttered a silent prayer for Hakmil; his hand was clenched into a fist and brought up to his twitching lips.

The squadron traversed several empty streets; crumbled, desiccated buildings loomed around every corner. It was a reflection of their evacuation zone, yet to their dismay, the damage was less significant. For every home that had been reduced to rubble, there were three or four still standing; if abandoned and gathering dust. There were also far less corpses mixed in with the debris.

When everyone felt they were far enough inside enemy territory, the squadron slowed down in pace.

"C-commander?" asked Kobina, in a muted voice, trying to regain his breath.

"Keep your voice low. You have permission to speak," Essayn responded in a much quieter tone.

"Where are we heading? Weren't we supposed to secure territory?"

"We need to find a base or munitions stockpile and either secure it or destroy it. That is correct."

"What happens afterwards?"

"We hold out until back up arrives."

"When will that happen? We were lucky to make it through the Joldies' defence."

"Then we need to make the most of our time here."

"So… we're not going to make it back…"

In the crimson moonlight of the second season's moon; everyone glanced over at Kobino, who was at the back of the group. All except Urshan, who kept his eyes on the road ahead. Gudemsha held a look of shame or disappointment, whilst Irralla and Essayn displayed stony expressions.

"I'm revoking your right to speak," Essayn ordered.

The squad found an abandoned home down a short cul-de-sac. Its position would keep them secluded. Gudemsha, with his impressive bulk, kicked the front door. It flew off its hinges. Inside, they set up camp for the night; Gudemsha replacing the door as best he could.

They made a small fire in what appeared to be the living room. Suddenly, Essayn spoke whilst gazing at the fire, to anyone who was listening. "Our generals and Captains are idiots…"

"What do you mean?" asked Irralla.

"They can spot weakness in the enemy line, yet they can't plan ahead to save the lives of their soldiers. It's like they see a chunk of gold, but have no idea what to do with it or how to invest it," Essayn shook his head. "Did you know I'm leading this squadron because I survived four days' worth of the front line?"

"Most of us are here because we outlived our brethren," said Urshan.

"Which reminds me. You don't seem comfortable around the reanimations. Why?" Essayn asked.

Urshan exhaled harshly. "It is a combination of what my mother taught me and what my father went through."

No one said anything until Irralla spoke up. "We're listening."

Urshan's focus remained on the fire. "My father had avoided conscription until I was ten. He was literally dragged out of our home and sent to the front line. A year later he was dead. Myself and my mother wept at the letter sent through our post, not just from the news but from the form that came with it."

"The permission form..." Essayn said with dour emotion.

"My mother denied the military permission to resurrect my father to further serve their cause; something that didn't endure her to the neighbours. When I was old enough to join the army, I did so. Then... I met my commanding general who told me he knew my father." Urshan glanced over to Essayn. "And how my father had served the army well in death."

Gudemsha and Irralla closed their eyes and grunted in self-shame.

Urshan continued. "The military ignored my mother's request. If it hadn't been for Hakmil, I would have given up trying to survive this long."

"You were close to Hakmil?" Gudemsha asked.

A faint smile appeared on Urshan's face. "It's a shame none of you had a chance to meet him. He was a lot like you, Gudemsha."

"What, fat and enjoyed blowing things up?" Gudemsha commented whilst grabbing his gut.

Everyone, including Kobino, chuckled.

Urshan gently shook his head. "I meant he was always ready with a joke in a dire situation."

"I try my best," Gudemsha patted his belly. "Speaking of which, I was really close to landing a gig at the Bargo Bein before I was enlisted."

"Wait- you were a stand-up comedian and you were going to play at the Bargo Bein?" said Irralla with renewed attention.

"I did stand-up at a few bars, then the bartender asked me what I'll be having…"

There was the sound of a *guffaw* but silence aside from that.

"I'll admit I'm out of practise. The war will do that to you."

"It's good to hear someone had a good life before the call to war," said Irralla.

Kobino went to utter something but stopped himself.

"You have permission to speak, Kobino. I merely didn't have an answer to your question earlier," said Essayn, placing a hand on Kobino's shoulder.

"Th-Thank you sir," Kobino said with a smile. He turned to Irralla. "I never had the chance to ask this when we served on the front line but; what was your life like before the war?"

Irralla grunted and shook her head. "I didn't have one. No job prospects, no father, and a mother who would have worked herself into an early grave had I not left the house when I did." She interlocked her hands behind her head and leaned back against the wall. "My last words to her were 'you deserve better'." She sniffed aggressively. "What about you, Koby? How was your life before the military?"

"Oh, erm… it was… simple."

"How so?" asked Essayn.

"I woke up in the morning, went to work, had lunch, worked some more, went home, had dinner-"

"I think we get the idea," said Irralla holding up her hand. "Did you enjoy your job?"

Kobino glanced around sheepishly. All eyes were on him. He hesitated for a moment before responding. "It was... not that interesting."

"Do you prefer it to being here?" asked Gudemsha.

Kobino felt all the eyes in the room fall upon him. He rubbed his wrists, brought his knees closer to his chest and kept gazing at the fire. "I... umm. That is-"

Essayn stood up and stretched, grunting and interrupting Kobino. "Grmm, we should turn in for the night," he said as he stomped out the fire. "We rise at first light."

Irralla volunteered to take first watch. From then until the break of dawn, everyone took two-hour shifts, keeping an eye out of the ground floor window.

Gudemsha lay with his hands behind his head, Urshan, Kobino and Essayn slept on their sides peacefully whilst Irralla cradled her rifle when she slept. The gun was unloaded, but two shells were kept nearby.

The night passed with the emergence of the rouge-tinted clouds of dawn.

No incidents.

*

The squad had been walking for an hour before Urshan spoke up.

"Forgive my questioning, commander, but… where are we going?"

"We're heading to an enemy base," Essayn responded, his voice weary.

"Only we've visited this road twice."

Essayn's voice broke with frustration. "Alright, so my sense of direction isn't perfect. By all means take the lead, if you wish."

The team turned a corner.

"No sir," said Urshan.

More blank, littered roads.

"As long as we find something soon, I'm not complaining. I have an itchy trigger finger," said Irralla.

"I second that," said Gudemsha.

The team turned another corner…

…straight into the sight of a group of soldiers, all male and clad in crisp white military uniform and armour plated fezzes. They were mid-march but slowing down, their rifles held high, fingers on the triggers.

Everyone's weapons were readied and aimed in a rush. Shouting and yelling ensued, with neither side listening.

Kobino's rifle trembled in his hand; he dropped to one knee to steady his aim.

The air erupted with the sound of gunfire.

Flecks of blood flew through the air from where lead bullets made burning craters in flesh.

Smoke mixed in with dust, kicked up by the impact of falling bodies.

And when the storm of screams and slaughter subsided, the ground was littered with empty shell casings and the still forms of the fallen. Both light brown and white uniforms lay strewn in the dirt.

Silence fell with them.

Time continued onwards, though not for the eight that lay dead.

The other two opened their eyes.

*

Kobino blinked rapidly, his ears ringing above all other sounds. His eyes bounced around, trying to survey his surroundings whilst he remained on his back. He remained prone and listened; nothing but the wind and far distant gunfire. When he was sure he was alone, he tried to move. His left shoulder wouldn't respond and at first felt like dead weight.

Then the pain kicked in.

He gasped and gingerly prodded the hole in in his shoulder; he couldn't tell if there was a bullet lodged in the muscle tissue or if the shot had penetrated through the bone and out the other side. Regardless, the wound seeped blood.

Kobino fetched a roll of bandage dressing and wrapped it around his shoulder using one arm and his teeth. The procedure was awkward and took way too much time; sweat beaded on his forehead. When he had finished, he looked around.

Kobino had to fight back tears.

Essayn, Gudemsha, Irralla and Urshan were all lying on the ground, unmoving. Essayn and Irralla had been shot through the head and Urshan through the heart, whilst Gudemsha's bloody arms were clutching his stomach. He had been gut shot and bled out while Kobino was unconscious. Thankfully the TNT Gudemsha had been carrying in his backpack hadn't been targeted, saving the ground from becoming a black crater and painting it with semi-vaporised entrails.

Kobino grabbed his rifle and got to his feet. He staggered over to the other group of bodies; the Jolduru enemy, their white uniforms displaying the gore in a more macabre fashion.

*"What am I doing? Do I carry out the mission by myself? Where by the gods were we even going?"*

Konbino gazed down at the bodies of the Jolduru enemy, unthinking yet unable to keep his attention on any of them.

Suddenly a rifle sprung up. Kobino aimed his own at the soldier; the tips of their bayonets inches from their faces.

The soldier had bullets in his knee and shoulder. His breathing was laboured and sweat was pouring from his face. He had a black goatee with grey mixed in. His birth emblem ran across the tops of his eyebrows.

Time crawled to a stop as Kobino and the soldier stared each other down, rifles armed and fingers tight around the triggers. The rifles were slightly different in design; Kobino's had a maple stock whilst the soldier's had teak. Kobino's barrel was also a little thinner.

"We seem to be at a stalemate," said the soldier.

"W-Why haven't you pulled the trigger already?" Kobino responded.

"We're both dead either way. You won't last long in this territory."

"Then why don't we just… put down our rifles?"

The soldier exhaled. His weapon dropped to the ground. Kobino flopped down to a seated position.

"Only a rookie would suggest peace in the middle of a battle."

"Look around you!" Kobino snapped. "The battle's over. My friends are dead, your friends are dead…"

"What was your mission?"

"What? Why should I tell you that?"

"Humour a dying man, why don't you?"

Kobino closed his eyes and shook his head. "We broke through a weak point in the enemy's defensive line. Our mission was to enter Jolduru territory, find an enemy camp and secure it."

The soldier let out a humourless laugh. "Typical short-sighted Galhadeen military tactics."

"At least our armies contain female soldiers and not slaves."

"And what of those undying abominations that serve your armies without question?"

"You speak as if you have the high ground in this argument?"

"We protect our women from the horrors of war, so that they may live and raise children in peace."

"Is that all they're good for? Breeding more soldiers for war?"

"Better that than violating the sanctity of life and death. Do the reanimated even get a choice in the matter?"

Kobino hesitated. "They can't feel pain and they originally signed up to serve. In life and death."

"You necromancers are truly despicable."

"You sexist, slave owners aren't any different. Speaking of which, how do you feel about using slaves for cannon fodder?"

"We feed and train those who are willing to fight and we do this very well, thanks to our superior military tact and funding. Something your generals and captains clearly lack."

Kobino went silent, tired of the bickering.

He changed the subject. "What was your team's mission?"

The soldier grunted. "We were sent to patch up the 'weak link' in our line. It appears…" The soldier grimaced and struggled to speak.

"What's wrong?"

"Could you perhaps patch up my wounds?"

"Why? You're the enemy?"

"And right now, I'm the only person alive to talk to… there's a first aid kit there."

The soldier titled his head towards a small satchel on the body of one of his comrades.

Kobino knelt down and fished around inside the satchel; he found a roll of bandages and a small bottle of disinfectant.

Kobino crawled over and treated the soldier's wounds. He could see the bullets had passed through.

The soldier remained expressionless and didn't flinch or grunt during the treatment.

"What's your name?" Kobino asked whilst bandaging the soldier's shoulder.

"Faraksem…"

"I'm Kobino," he said quickly and without tone.

Once Faraksem had been treated to the best of Kobino's ability, he shuffled over to the nearest, most intact, stone wall. Kobino joined him and they sat in silence for many minutes.

Kobino finally broke the uncomfortable tension. "So, what will happen when they find out your mission is a failure?"

"They will send reinforcements, but they may take a few days to arrive."

"Will they shoot you for your failure?"

"You assume our military to be merciless?" Faraksem shook his head. "No, once I am back on my feet, I will return to the front line. We need every unit, every man, every soldier."

"Then why not include women in your ranks?"

Faraksem snorted. "I don't give orders or run the militia, and even if I did, I still wouldn't let a woman anywhere near the battlefield."

"Why is that difficult for your people to understand?"

"Our people? Don't insult me by claiming we're a different race of people. And by that suggestion, why do you not see necromancy as a crime against nature?"

"We see it as overcoming something that has plagued humanity since the very beginning; death. Haven't you been aggrieved by death and wanted to see someone you love come back?"

"Not as the abominations you throw onto the battlefield. I haven't even mentioned the children you use for war."

"You mean the messengers? They're orphans with no other place to go. Our army feeds them and gives them somewhere warm to sleep."

"That's if they ever see a bed before a bullet enters their head."

Kobino went silent for a few seconds. "We're back to bickering again... remind me why I tried to keep you alive?"

"If you tire of my company, then leave. You are in a decent enough condition to move, yes?"

Kobino sighed. "And where would I go? I'm knee-deep in enemy territory and can't remember how I got here."

"Not my issue."

Kobino looked over at his fallen comrades. His chest tightened.

"You see the woman amongst my comrades?" Kobino pointed to Irralla's body.

Faraksem glanced over then looked away, sneering in disgust. "Are you proud she joined in wars of men?"

"She'd spent most of her time working munitions; preparing weapons, hand-loading shells. She couldn't wait to join the front lines. I'd never seen someone so eager to put a bullet through a Joldie's head." Kobino fixed Faraksem a stern look. "I couldn't be prouder; she died fighting for what she believed in. Can the women of your city say the same?"

Faraksem didn't answer. Unsmiling, he pulled out a rolled cigarette from his pocket and lit it with a match. After taking a drag, he finally responded.

"If you're trying to convert me to your twisted way of thinking, then you clearly don't know how this war started."

Silence dulled the mood for the next hour. The sun had broken the skyline, north of the pair's position, giving the very beyond hues of heated tin. Kobino ate from another can of his rations; spiced beans. Faraksem had chain-smoked at least three cigarettes by the time they started talking again. The wind blew the overpowering stench of tobacco over Kobino's clothes.

"So what made you join the army?" Kobino asked.

"What other reason should there be? National pride. I joined the moment I was old enough. Better than being a delivery boy."

"I was conscripted. I didn't have a choice."

"You were happy rolling around in the mud or begging?"

"I had a job… as a postman."

"And that was far more exciting than fighting for your country?"

"I… I didn't want to die. And I was happy with my simple life. War terrified me."

Faraksem took a moment to absorb Kobino's explanation. He reacted with a small smile. "Then I'm impressed you've made it this far."

"Thank you."

Neither man looked at each other. They stared at various parts of the scenery in front of them; keeping their sight away from the corpses. Yet there was nothing to see; maybe the odd stray cat or dog once in a while, and one could only look at an abandoned building, demolished or otherwise, so many times.

"How are you? Are your wounds healing?" Kobino asked.

Faraksem shuffled from his seated position. He gave his bandaged shoulder a slow wind up. "Your first aid isn't bad." He tried to stand, but winced and exhaled heavily through his nose. "But I will not be going anywhere soon."

"I know the feeling." Kobino peered up at the cloudless sky; hints of a content smile prodded him in the cheek. "I doubt I'll ever leave this place now."

Faraksem hesitated to speak for a second. He finally grunted, then spoke. "Turn left around that corner and keep going straight. Take the road right at the end and keep going until you hit a crossroads, then-"

"What are you saying?"

"I'm giving you directions on how to get out of here."

"I will not leave you."

Faraksem's face scrunched in disappointment and frustration. "Then you will die here. Don't be an idiot, run."

"I may despise your way of thinking, but I cannot and will not leave the wounded. Besides, where will your directions take me?"

"Another chink in our defensive lines armour. You could make it…"

"If I am to die, I shall do so in company. With allies."

"Don't be such a pacifist. This war has no place for them. And I'm not your ally."

"Acquaintance, then."

Faraksem huffed. "I'll never understand you Galhads"

"I could never make sense of a Joldie either. May I change the subject?"

"Go ahead," Faraksem said with a dismissive wave of his hand.

"Were they your friends?" Kobino nodded to the deceased Jolduru soldiers.

"I never made many friends during basic training. Except one... the body closest to me. His name was Dohkeem. He was polite and protected those he cared about. He was also a pretty good cook. His curried goat was, if you'll pardon the circumstantial pun, to die for."

Kobino let out a little chuckle. "Sounds fantastic. I heard Gudemsha was a good cook but I never got to try anything he made. It's funny how the army is supposed to break you down and build you up again in their image. But you never forget what makes you yourself."

"You're getting a little too soppy for my taste," Faraksem said with a disturbed frown.

A few rats scurried from cracks and holes in the buildings around Kobino and Faraksem. The vermin took a keen interest in the greying, visibly veined corpses.

Kobino crawled over to his former friends, waving his cap rifle in an attempt to disperse the carrion feeders. Faraksem did the same.

"It won't be long before the flies surround them," Faraksem said in a hoarse voice.

"I just can't let my friends be disgraced like this."

"Interesting, coming from a Galhad."

Kobino loaded a cap into his rifle, aimed it skyward and fired. The swarm dispersed. Kobino moved onto his knees and gave his shoulder a turn. He felt small painful rips in his flesh and growled in frustration.

"You've just given away our position," said Faraksem.

"I'm sorry, but I am past the point of caring. You need medical attention."

"They won't arrest you as a prisoner of war. If we're found, they will shoot you."

Kobino laid his rifle on the ground. "So be it."

Within a minute, Kobino could hear the *thump* of marching feet. He looked at the brown-red ground and closed his eyes in prayer. Faraksem ordered him to hide, to run. His orders turned to begs.

Kobino blocked out all sound and focused on his thoughts. He prayed for his deceased friends, so that they may find peace. He prayed to Shaelam, his people's god of mercy and apologised to the other gods for his mistakes.

His meditation was interrupted by the butt of a gun, smacking him in the side of the head. A group of four Jolduru soldiers stood before him. Two aimed rifles at his face whilst the other two attended to Faraksem.

"I've patched him up as best-" Kobino began, but was interrupted by a kick to the gut.

"Be quiet, scum."

Faraksem's voice rose in his best attempt at gaining attention and command. "Please, spare him. He saved my life."

"You know we cannot do that," said one of the soldiers attending to Faraksem, before nodding to one of the men above Kobino.

Kobino smiled through a swollen cheek. *"Thank you, friend."*

Not for the first time that day, a gun was fired. It discharged a bullet into Kobino's head, spreading a spatter of blood across the ground.

Faraksem's eyes stayed on Kobino, his expression stuck in a twisted mixture of horror and regret.

He closed his eyes as he was moved onto a gurney of wood and fabric.

*

Faraksem awoke in a hospital. Darkening orange sunlight flickered through the wooden shutters of the room. A woman in a thick, ankle-length white dress and cowl scrubbed the floors on her hands and knees. The walls were made of pale brown stone, chipped and cracked in areas. A tiny bedside table and a thin wooden chair accompanied every bed in the room, of which there were six.

A man with a very well-kept full-face beard marched into the room. His white uniform jacket was adorned with tin medals and stripes. He clicked his fingers twice to the cleaning lady, who picked up her brush and bucket then left the room without a word.

The officer pulled up a chair and sat at Faraksem's bedside. The officer's birth emblems, now more visible, were a pair of curved tendrils around circles, like licks of flame around one side of a sun.

The emblems were positioned upon either sides of his temple.

"General Mithuran," said Faraksem, sitting up straight.

"Good to see you conscious, Faraksem." The General's voice was, in the fashion of a typical high commanding officer, deep and demanding of obedience.

"Yes, sir."

"I need a report of just what the devil happened to you and your squad." There was no hint of amusement in his voice.

"We encountered another squad of Galhad's that had broken through a weak link in our defensive line; the one we were sent to defend."

"And what of the surviving Galhad who was found with you?"

"He saved my life."

Mithuran sniffed and stroked his beard. "Why didn't you shoot him?"

Faraksem struggled to find an answer. "Sir?" was all he could manage.

"At some point you had the enemy in your crosshairs. Yet you hesitated to shoot him over the course of, what five hours? Why?"

"S-Sir, he saved my life, so that I might-"

"Slay the enemy, that is all. Basic training should have taught you that even if you are bleeding out through your mangled guts, you shoot the enemy. To the very last breath, you fight."

"Forgive me sir, I-"

"Don't you dare beg me for forgiveness; it is not my place to give it. You will be held before a tribunal in a few days' time. The best you can expect is a lashing and a return to the front line."

Faraksem didn't respond. General Mithuran stood up and put away his chair.

"Personally, I hope you do. It'll make up for your pitiful performance. Dismissed."

The general marched out of the bay.

## Acknowledgements

To Kelly for beta reading this book.
To Kyle Martin (Krimson Rogue) for the second beta read.
To Mai's writing class for giving me an outlet to be creative.
To Shauni Lane thrice times over for making my maps look professional and not awful MS paint quality splodges.
To Charlie Vaughan, who made the first front cover, your work is truly buckworthy.
To Daniell Fine for the current cover.
To Megan Whiting for the secondary edit.
To family and friends for listening to me ramble on about my past, present and future stories for the Orran adventure series.
And to Stacey Rezvan for saving me a lot of trouble…

Cheers.

## About the author

Timothy Darrell Howard is a man of many former hobbies. These include pro-wrestling, bass guitar, brewing, body building, learning German, growing a beard, stop motion film and motorcycle club member. He sings at folk gatherings and started writing books in hopes of one day finding true love… or some such malarkey.

Half of his first draft for this book was written inebriated.

## Other works

If you enjoyed this book and want to read more adventures contained within the world of Orran, check out the authors previous titles.

### Clockwork Hearts

### The Buried Man

Check out orranadventures.wordpress.com for future titles.

Follow me on Twitter: @TimothyDHCB

Made in the USA
Lexington, KY
22 May 2018